## "Oh, that feels delicious."

Shelby sighed in contentment as Jake massaged her right foot.

"Have you ever heard of shiatsu?" His efforts were now focused on her toes.

She smiled. "No, but I think I've ordered it in a Japanese restaurant by accident."

Jake ran his thumbs along the aching base of her heel, and she almost purred. "I'm doing a survey of your anatomy. Shiatsu is an Oriental massage discipline. Practitioners say that each portion of your foot corresponds to another part of your body." He resumed kneading her sole with great seriousness.

"Heaven," Shelby cooed. "What part of my body is that?"

Jake looked up with a secret smile and didn't answer.

We're pleased to introduce **Katherine Kendall** to Temptation readers in this, her first book. Since college, Katherine's worked her way through an eclectic assortment of jobs, looking for one that would pay her to indulge in romantic daydreams. She finally returned to writing, her childhood passion, and at about the same time started studying the cello. She says she was surprised to discover that not only were people willing to pay her to write, they were also willing to pay her *not* to play the cello. *We* don't know about her musical ability, but her talent for creating symphonious romance fiction is considerable.

Single, Katherine lives in Portland, Maine. Though she's found the man of her dreams, she explains, he's still officially a "significant other."

# The Midas Touch

## KATHERINE KENDALL

# *Harlequin Books*

x

TORONTO • NEW YORK • LONDON
AMSTERDAM • PARIS • SYDNEY • HAMBURG
STOCKHOLM • ATHENS • TOKYO • MILAN

For Sue and Rog,
with love

Published December 1988

ISBN 0-373-25331-1

# 1

ONCE AGAIN HE HAD ELUDED HER.

Shelby Haynes glanced at the luminous dial of her waterproof watch and mentally computed the amount of air left in her tanks. She still had plenty of oxygen, but the water of the North Atlantic was freezing, especially at this depth. How much longer could she ignore the numbing chill penetrating her wet suit?

*Damn it, Harold. I'm just trying to help.*

One last time Shelby scanned the area through the viewfinder of her underwater camera. Peering upward, she could see the bubbles from her regulator become bright pearls as they rose toward dappled sunlight.

There was no sign of Harold anywhere. Most of the time he was downright eager to have his picture taken.

Harold was what marine scientists called a "friendly"—a whale who was unusually gregarious around human beings. Today, however, he'd taken one look at her and steamed away at a speed she could not match. She hoped it was just a game of hide-and-seek, and nothing more serious.

*Harold, come out and show your face, so at least I know you're all right!*

Something was killing the whale population that fed in these waters off the tip of Cape Cod, and it was her job to find out what it was—a job that was proving all but impossible. Just two days earlier another humpback calf had washed up on the beach near Provincetown, barely able to breathe, and although the Safeseas Institute was doing all it could to save the animal, the prognosis was bleak.

With a quick kick that expressed more than a little annoyance, Shelby began her slow ascent, ready to call it a day. Suddenly she felt a wrenching blow against her back. The impact forced air from her lungs in an explosion of bubbles.

Shark! she thought instantly, as fear iced her veins. Without waiting to give the unseen predator a second opportunity, she took two powerful strokes with her flippers.

Nothing happened. She was merely treading water, unable to move forward, unable to move upward. Whatever it was, it was holding her. But at least it wasn't a shark.

Only then did she catch sight of a thin steel cable snaking upward through the water at a forty-five-degree angle before disappearing out of sight. Awkwardly she reached back over her shoulder, feeling for her scuba equipment. Sure enough, the cable was tightly wedged between her two tanks, but as encumbered as she was, she could barely reach the line, let alone free herself.

A growing fury began to eclipse her fear. These were supposed to be protected waters! And this was certainly no ordinary fishing line that had her hooked as if she were a marlin.

Before she could decide on her next move, the line suddenly snapped tight, wrenching from her grasp. Shelby felt herself being pulled, like a submerged water-skier, toward the surface. The force of the water tore at her mask. Clutching at it, she lost her grip on the camera. She made one desperate effort to catch it, but the camera sank slowly away, like a paper airplane tossed from a great height, until it was swallowed by the gloom.

Anger seared her. Two thousand dollars' worth of Safeseas equipment, lost forever on the ocean floor. Someone would pay for this. She'd see to it!

Assuming, that was, she got out of this ridiculous predicament in one piece. Thank goodness she'd been at a shallow depth and had had some time to decompress during her ascent. Getting the bends could be deadly; on that score, at least, she'd been lucky. If they continued to pull her at this speed, she would break the surface in thirty seconds or so, and with any luck at all, her colleague Sam would be relatively close at hand in their inflatable Zodiac. If there was any trouble, surely he would hear her cries for help.

Above her the sunlight was streaming past, a dappled kaleidoscope of white foam and pale blue sky. As she surfaced, dropping her mouth piece from angrily clenched teeth, the line went slack, and she felt a blast of warm air on her forehead and cheeks. Shelby began to tread water, trying to lift her head high enough above the light chop to locate her tormentor. She pulled up her face mask, blinking in the unfiltered light that accosted her eyes.

A swell caught her and lifted her to its crest, where she caught sight of the imposing bulk of a seventy-foot cabin cruiser. Perhaps a half-dozen people waved to her from the stern, cheering raucously. Two of them fished up the end of the line and began to haul her in by hand.

"It's a mermaid!" one of the onlookers yelled.

Shelby was close enough now to see their faces. Five men and one woman: tourists out for a day of fishing, no doubt. Even so, she wondered, seething with rage, why the cable? And what were those crates she could see lashed down to the deck?

"You okay?" a young man called as she neared the black hull. Above her a collection of sunburned faces peered down expectantly.

"I've been better."

"We must have snagged her tanks," the young woman suggested.

"I hate to interrupt your little fishing expedition," Shelby said evenly, "but could someone give me a hand here?"

Before anyone could answer, she heard a loud splash, followed by a surge that caught her off guard. Temporarily submerged, she felt a power not her own gently lift her until her head was once again above water. She noticed a firm pressure on her hips and reached down to discover two large, very strong hands grasping her confidently.

Surfacing again, Shelby spluttered and blinked, not sure whether she was more annoyed by the saltwater she'd inhaled or by the presumptuous stranger trying to play lifeguard. After all, she spent a good portion of her life in the water. She needed rescuing by these lunatics like she needed a hole in the head! Twisting halfway around, she glimpsed only a bare shoulder and upper arm, thickly muscled and sunbronzed. The would-be rescuer still grasped her altogether too familiarly from behind.

"Come here often?" a husky bass drawled in her ear.

Shelby wrenched her hips violently in an effort to escape his grip—no easy task while trying to keep her mouth above water.

"Take your hands off me," she said with all the threat she could muster.

"Suit yourself." There was an unmistakable hint of the Southwest in his voice. The pressure of his touch evaporated at once, and with one powerful stroke he pulled past her to the side of the cruiser.

Shelby blinked, squeezing the water from her eyes. With one gloved hand she smoothed her hair back from her forehead to get a better look at the aspiring lifesaver bobbing before her in the chilly green water.

His dark eyes were filled with the same amusement she'd heard in his voice, and she felt a strange flicker of recognition. Unruly waves of jet-black hair hung low on his brow, and beneath a neatly trimmed mustache his lips curled in an ironic half smile. Her gaze traveled from the hard, tanned planes of his jaw back to his eyes. They softened him a bit, she decided, made him seem less . . . sure of himself.

Before Shelby could speak, a strong swell forced her against the side of the boat, burying her in a foamy backwash. Again the man's arm found her, reaching around below her tanks to lift her into the air. Against her neck she felt a sandpaper jaw and the warmth of his breath on her throat.

"Actually," Shelby said, "I *do* know how to swim. I think you can safely let me go now."

"I could—" he said, grinning slyly "—but it's a long way back to shore, and I have the only boat around."

"It's only three miles. I'll take my chances."

His laugh was sudden and warmly genuine. "You know, I believe you would." He released her and called for a ladder to be lowered over the side of the boat.

"Is she a keeper?" a voice inquired gaily.

"Absolutely." Shelby's companion nodded toward the ladder. "Would you do me the honor of climbing aboard the *Questor*?"

"I won't be able to climb anywhere until you undo your handiwork."

"Glad to, ma'am."

He swam behind her and examined the line. Grunting with effort, he managed after several tries to set her free.

"You're welcome," he remarked while she silently considered several options for extracting revenge.

This seagoing cowboy expected her to thank him?

"Forgive me," she exclaimed with feigned sweetness. "You Southern gentlemen are used to more polite behavior from women, aren't you? Well, I want to thank you for dragging me around Stellwagen Bank and then being courteous enough to cut me loose. Really I do."

She paddled briskly over to the chrome ladder, where several willing hands were extended to help her with her heavy tanks. Even without the scuba tanks themselves, the rest of her gear—fins, weight belt and the tight-fitting wet suit—made climbing difficult.

Behind her a rich male voice tinged with amusement called, "Greg, where's your sense of chivalry? Help our prize catch aboard."

Shelby formed a retort, but an unexpected wave of fatigue assailed her, buckling her knees. It wasn't surprising, now that the adrenaline was beginning to wear off. She'd been exhausted, anyway, and now, without the buoyancy of the water, it was hitting her full force. Once she got her second wind, she would set things straight.

Safe on deck, she was at once surrounded by crew members. Someone handed her a towel, and she pressed its reassuring warmth against her face. Shelby searched the horizon for landmarks. The Provincetown tower was farther off to starboard than she'd expected. No wonder she couldn't see Sam and the Zodiac; she'd strayed far from the area where she'd entered the water. In another few minutes Sam would begin to worry. He might even try to go in after her.

"Here, here, young lady. You look a bit green around the gills. You'd better have yourself a seat and catch your wind."

Shelby focused on a bearded, middle-aged man whose belly betrayed a long love affair with beer. Gratefully she sank into a deck chair, kicking off her flippers and removing her face mask.

A younger man presented her with a mug of steaming coffee. Soon her fingers had been warmed back to sensibility by the heat of the cup, and the radiance of the sun on the teakwood deck had thawed her toes. She supposed they were trying to be nice, but they had also carelessly endangered her and lost one very expensive camera, and she was not about to let them off the hook.

After a few moments the crewmen who'd been huddled around her fell back to make way for the man obviously responsible for the entire fiasco. There could be no doubt that the dark-eyed stranger was in command; he did not seem like the sort of man who had ever been in less than total command.

"Here you go, Captain," someone called, throwing him a large blue beach towel. He draped it casually over his broad tawny shoulders and smiled thoughtfully down at Shelby.

"Okay, guys," came the now-familiar voice, warm and velvet edged, "back to work. Let's give our friend here a chance to catch her breath." He turned to the man in a Red Sox baseball cap who had brought her the coffee. "How about some coffee for me, J.B.? Or am I not pretty enough?"

"No one is prettier than the person who signs my paychecks, Captain." He offered a mock salute and headed toward the galley. The rest of the crew dispersed, buzzing purposefully around the deck, which was littered with pallets, small crates and an assortment of machinery.

Shelby rose to her feet, determined, despite her fatigue, to meet her host on equal terms. That was possible while floating in the ocean, but here on deck the man towered over her. The sun was behind him and she felt completely enveloped in his shadow.

Glancing over his powerfully built body, her gaze was drawn to a pair of bleached cutoffs that had obviously seen better days. The wet denim clung to his tightly muscled upper thighs like a second skin. Sunlight caught the beaded water on his arms and chest and turned the drops into tiny blazing diamonds. She surveyed the expanse of his chest, its firmness softened only by the glistening dark hair that traced an entrancing line down his hard brown abdomen.

"I think you have me at a bit of a disadvantage," he said, crossing his arms over his chest with an amused stare.

"Funny," Shelby retorted, "a few minutes back I was thinking the same thing about you."

His grin was disarmingly boyish. "Actually I was referring to that rubber armor you're wearing. It makes me feel a bit . . . underdressed. Perhaps you'd like to slip into something more comfortable? Or at least out of something uncomfortable?"

"I'm perfectly comfortable, Mr.—"

"Captain," he corrected.

"Captain what, might I ask?"

"Captain Bligh," a merry feminine voice offered. Shelby turned to see the darkly tanned young woman she had glimpsed from the water.

"I heard you were growling for coffee," the woman said, handing him a mug.

"Thanks, Janine." He took a sip from the cup while keeping his attention on Shelby.

"Would you care for a refill?" the woman asked kindly.

"Thanks, no." Shelby returned her smile. "This isn't exactly a social call." She turned back to her host. "You're a veritable Welcome Wagon, Captain. Where are the cookies and cucumber sandwiches?"

"Sorry, no cucumbers today, but we do have some stale doughnuts. I'm sure Janine would be glad to—"

"That's wonderfully gracious of you, Captain. But all I need is a ride back to my Zodiac."

"You mean you didn't swim all the way out here? I'm disappointed." He nodded to the crew woman. "Janine, please tell Greg to turn back toward that launch we passed a mile or so back."

"Sure thing," she answered, turning on her heel and heading toward the bridge.

"I should have been up five minutes ago," Shelby muttered, checking her watch. "Sam—my assistant—is probably worried sick about me."

"Worried about you? Somehow I doubt that."

"I beg your pardon?"

"I think the only person in any danger out there was me, when I made the unfortunate error of thinking you needed to be rescued."

"Yes, I can handle myself in the water."

"Oh, I'm convinced of that." He took another sip of coffee. "You know, it's a bit of a trip back to your boat, and that suit must be getting hot."

"You seem terribly concerned with my comfort," she said dubiously. But the truth was, her suit was becoming unbearably hot. The midday sun was conspiring with her host to raise her body temperature to well over 98.6 degrees.

"I can assure you, my motives are mostly pure," he protested. "I would hate to have any guest on my boat swelter. And of course," he added roguishly, "I would hate to have to remember you in my dreams as a gorgeous blonde with the body of a snow tire."

"Well," Shelby admitted reluctantly, "I am a little warm." She settled into a deck chair and began to remove the top half of her wet suit.

The captain leaned against the railing, sipping his coffee, watching her with barely suppressed amusement.

"Don't you have something better to do?" Shelby grunted with the effort of pulling off the rest of her second skin.

"Nope."

She tried to writhe free while maintaining some level of dignity.

It was easier with someone assisting, but she wasn't about to ask for help. "I'm so glad I could provide a morning's cheap entertainment for you, Captain." At least she'd made it past her hips.

He knelt beside her, setting aside his mug. "You know, you might try asking for help now and then," he suggested softly. "Though I realize you certainly don't *need* to be rescued."

Was he reading her mind?

Without waiting for an answer he began carefully peeling back the tight rubber encasing her right leg, slowly exposing a smooth thigh and long muscular calf.

Shelby swallowed her sharp retort as he began baring her other leg. For a brief moment his fingertips grazed the tender flesh along the inside of her thigh.

A soft gasp escaped her lips as something—a question, a challenge, perhaps—flew between them like lightning along a steel cable. By the time Shelby had registered its effect in the pit of her stomach, he had removed the remaining few inches of her suit.

He tossed the wet suit on the deck and stood, hands on hips. "There now—" he looked down at her "—that's much better."

Shelby was overcome by a sudden longing for the comforting rubber camouflage. Beneath her host's unsettling gaze, she felt that her yellow maillot left little to the imagination.

But then, the same could be said of his cutoffs.

She stifled the errant thought and reminded herself she was this man's most unwilling guest.

"Now that I meet the requirements of your dress code," she began, "I have a few questions for you." She folded her arms across the gentle swell of her breasts, jaw set firmly.

"Fire away." He reached for another deck chair and settled across from her, stroking his mustache as he eyed her expectantly.

There was an air of nonchalance about him that left her feeling like a teacher chastising an unrepentant schoolboy. The slightest hint of a devilish smile lurked at one corner of his mouth, threatening to erupt at any moment.

"For openers, just what the hell were you doing tearing through Stellwagen Bank with that . . . that ten-mile fishing line? I could have been killed!"

The amusement vanished from his features. "Look," he told her, voice muted, "I realize you had quite a scare out there, and I'm sorry. Really I am." When she didn't respond, he continued. "We just didn't expect anyone to be in the area. Most people go to the Y to swim laps. And I might point out that even a rank amateur knows enough to fly a diving flag."

Shelby grimaced. He was right about that much, at least. "Someone must have lost our flag the last time the boat was used. We didn't realize it until we were all the way out here. But when you passed my Zodiac, that should have been warning enough," she added hotly. "And besides, that's not the point!" Shelby pounded her fist on the chair arm with such force that she winced at the unexpected pain. "These are protected waters! If you and your drinking buddies want a prize for your mantel, go dynamite some pond. But play games in *my* ocean, friend, and it's *my* business."

"*Your* ocean, eh?" he mused, dark eyebrows cocked. "That's one deed I'd like to lay my hands on."

She'd had run-ins with this type before, the kind of man who thought the ocean was a sprawling adult playground, who had no respect for its laws or its fragility.

There was only one way to communicate with his breed.

"You know, Captain," she said with exaggerated calm, "I hope you keep a fair amount of change on board. I lost a two-thousand-dollar camera down there, and someone's going to pick up the tab." She paused, summoning an innocent smile. "Lawsuits can be so messy. Don't you agree?"

As she'd expected, her mention of the camera sparked an instant change in his demeanor. He leaned back in his chair, rubbing his jaw, his face a mask of wary skepticism. In spite of herself, she felt defensive.

"Let me make something abundantly clear, my little mermaid friend," he warned. "You lost a camera? Send me the bill. End of story. But don't go poking that charming little nose of yours around where it doesn't belong. What I'm doing here—" he waved toward the cabin "—is my business, not yours. The last place I want to see my face is on the cover of some supermarket tabloid. Tell your editor to stick with the traditional—three-headed offspring of Elvis, that sort of thing."

Shelby's jaw dropped in disbelief. What on earth was he accusing her of? She had begun to suspect that, whatever his physical blessings, the captain had been shortchanged in the brains department.

"You seem like a nice enough gal," he continued evenly. "Let's just forget this whole unfortunate run-in. You pretend you were just taking pictures of the fishies, and I'll pretend the district attorney's not a real good buddy of mine. Deal?"

"How dare you threaten me! And for your information, I *was* taking pictures of the 'fishies'!" Out of the corner of her eye she noticed a couple of crew members turning at the sound of her raised voice and whispering discreetly.

"Right. And I was just trolling for my supper."

Shelby stood abruptly, struggling to maintain some semblance of composure. "Listen," she insisted, adopting the tone she generally reserved for small children and lunatics, "in my twenty-nine years I have never read, let alone worked for, some supermarket tabloid."

His eyes narrowed doubtfully.

"Oh, all right, maybe I read the headlines while I'm waiting in line," she confessed. "What I want to know is why they'd consider you a worthy topic in the first place. After everything I've been through, I think you owe me that much."

His gaze bored into her as he engaged in some private debate. Seconds passed before he stood slowly, facing her. His broad brown chest rose and fell only inches from her touch.

Sighing heavily, he reached into the front pocket of his dilapidated cutoffs. The object he retrieved was a small plastic cube, an inch and a half on each side. Without a word he pressed it into Shelby's palm.

Inside, suspended and protected, was a thick gold coin with a hole bored in the middle.

"French," he offered by way of explanation. "1684." His voice was at once proud and self-deprecating. "My first. Some people carry a rabbit's foot. I lug this around."

The realization hit her with the force of a gale. Of course! The cable, the machinery, the crates on deck, the air of understated mystery... It had to be!

Before her stood the great treasure hunter from Texas, the man who had vowed to find the most fabled wreck in North America, the pirate ship *Evangeline*, which had sunk off Cape Cod in 1723. He'd been the talk of the town for months, but stubbornly elusive, invisible to the public eye.

Until now.

"So," she said slowly, "You are Jake Lawson." She shook her head, unable to reconcile the man before her with the image she had long ago formed in her mind.

"In the flesh. I suppose that comes as a big surprise to you?"

"Actually yes," Shelby remarked coolly. "You make Howard Hughes look gregarious. And you think I'm a reporter trying to get the scoop on your dig?"

Lawson crossed his arms over his chest. "You have a better story, no doubt?"

"I'm afraid you're not going to like it much. If I want to get the scoop on you, Captain Lawson, I won't need to sneak around to do it."

"Come again?"

Shelby extended her hand to him with a frosty smile. Lawson shook it, a bit hesitantly, watching her through veiled lids.

"I'm Shelby Haynes, Captain Lawson. Director of cetacean research—that means whales, incidentally—at the Safeseas Institute in Provincetown. I was filming a humpback whale named Harold when you so rudely interrupted me."

"Ah." A flicker of understanding swept over Lawson's chiseled features. "I don't suppose you'd be one of those overzealous types who kept this project tied up for months?"

"I'd hoped the state underwater archaeological board would show more consideration for the marine life you'll be jeopardizing, yes." She paused, waiting for the diatribe that undoubtedly would follow, but Lawson was silent.

A slow smile stirred on her lips. He didn't know!

"You have no idea who I am, do you?" Shelby asked coyly.

"Sure. You just told me. One of the whale nuts who cost me an arm and a leg in attorneys' fees."

She laughed brittlely. The state had stalled for months before giving approval to Lawson's search only last week. She'd been an outspoken opponent of his excavation, reasoning that the marine life in the area deserved protection, treasure or no treasure. Several whales had already perished from the mysterious illness; why, she'd argued, add insult to injury?

"In the end, we 'whale nuts' lost, Captain Lawson."

"I guess the state realized the whales were more endangered by the tourists out here than by one little search vessel."

"What the state realized," she retorted, "was how big its share of the pot would be, in the unlikely event that you find what you're looking for."

"And just what is it you think I'm looking for, Ms Hayes?"

"I don't suppose money has anything to do with your little hunt, does it?"

His smile was wry and knowing. "You're a cynic, Shelby Haynes."

"And you're a self-serving, opportunistic, greedy—"

"Captain?" called a questioning voice behind them.

"It's okay, Marcus," Lawson answered, glancing back. "Ms Haynes was just enumerating my many virtues. But I think I'm reasonably safe."

The grizzled older crewman lumbered up, shooting a curious glance in Shelby's direction. "We've spotted the Zodiac, Captain."

"Thank God," Shelby breathed with relief. In a few brief minutes Lawson had managed to drag her through the gamut of emotions, from terror to fury to something less easily labeled—something she preferred not to acknowledge. The remembered security of the Zodiac seemed heavenly by comparison.

She picked up her wet suit, which lay at her feet in a soggy heap, and moved to follow Marcus toward the stern.

"Wait." Lawson, solid as a stone statue, barred her path. "What is it?"

His eyes were riveted on her, challenging her to hear him out. "You're wrong about me, Ms Haynes. I'll do everything in my power to protect the whales while we excavate. I—" he hesitated, looking past her to the wind-whipped sea "—I really love this ocean."

The emotion in his voice touched her like a physical caress, but she did not respond. The man was a complete enigma—more than she wanted to tackle just now.

"And don't forget," he added, his tone brightening, "we'll have a scientist on board the whole time. The state's actually appointed a baby-sitter to be sure we behave ourselves."

Shelby waved to Sam in the Zodiac not far off starboard. "I know, Captain Lawson." She sighed softly. "And if today's any indication, I'm really going to have my hands full."

She was gratified to see his eyes widen in momentary shock, but he recovered quickly.

"Well, Ms Haynes," he said laconically, "I've had just about every kind of bad luck you can think of on this operation. I guess you can't make things any worse."

Shelby stepped over the side of the railing onto the ladder as the Zodiac pulled up beneath her. She paused for a moment and favored him with a determined smile.

"I wouldn't count on that, Captain Lawson."

# 2

IT WAS A GLORIOUS SUNDAY.

So glorious, in fact, that by noon Shelby was ready to abandon all hope of getting any more work done. She had spent the morning catching up on the paperwork she inevitably let slide each week: forms for this, more forms for that. But after a few hours she was famished, and far enough through her In basket to once again let things go.

She locked the front door of the small white building that housed the Safeseas office and stepped out into the street. It was, she had to admit, far too beautiful a day to remain cooped up in the office. More than one of her colleagues had chided her about her "workaholic" hours lately; maybe they had a point. But since her divorce two years earlier, she had made work the center of her existence. The fiasco of her marriage to Steve had taught her the importance of making a life that was truly her own.

The cobblestoned streets of Provincetown were gridlocked with pedestrians and automobiles moving at a careful crawl, but as she made her way through the throngs, she spotted a familiar face across the street.

Teresa Cabral waved. She was a volunteer for Safeseas who made her living weaving wonderful tapestries and wall hangings that she sold in local boutiques. Terry was seldom anything less than ebullient, but today her normally mischievous expression was subdued. As she waited for the traffic between them to clear, Shelby was struck by her closest friend's darkly sensuous eyes and the unselfconscious poise that made Terry look more like a descendant of Portuguese royalty than the daughter of an immigrant fisherman.

When the line of cars came to a stop, Terry threaded her way across the street.

"Hi, Terry. Heading downtown?"

"Yes, more or less." She seemed to be holding something back.

"Why do I get the feeling you've got some bad news to tell me?" Shelby asked as lightly as she could, though her intuition was sounding an alarm.

Teresa took Shelby's hand and pulled her out of the stream of pedestrians.

"I was just coming down to the office to tell you. I had the ship-to-shore radio on while I was cleaning my oven—now you know how I spend my day off. Anyway, the Coast Guard has spotted another dead whale. They're pretty sure it's a humpback, floating about two miles off Truro."

"Oh, no!" Shelby groaned, shaking her head in frustration.

"They can't really be sure when it will come ashore, or where, but I got hold of Dr. Tuan and Sam. Tuan said he would handle the follow-up."

"Thanks." Shelby nodded grimly.

They rejoined the crowd moving slowly down the gentle slope of Commercial Street.

"You know, Tuan told me last week that he thinks I'm overly emotional about these whale deaths," Shelby remarked evenly.

"I think we all are."

"Still, I'm a scientist first. He makes me feel defensive about showing my feelings."

"Tuan's a good vet. And he cares, too."

"He's a good vet," Shelby agreed, adding with a smile, "he's also a pain in the—"

"Derriere?" Teresa offered.

"Don't quote me on that. Lord knows I can't afford to lose him." Her face clouded. "Especially not now, with me off baby-sitting Captain Jake Almighty Lawson."

"Have you met him yet?"

"Oh, I met him, all right."

"And?" Teresa prodded, the mischievous glint returning to her eyes.

"And what?"

"Don't make me twist your arm, Shelby. What's he like?"

"He called me a cynic."

"Well, then, he's observant."

Shelby stopped suddenly, nearly colliding with a middle-aged man sporting a Hawaiian shirt and two cameras.

"I'm only cynical," she retorted with a smile, "when it's appropriate. And believe me, in the case of Jake Lawson, it's appropriate."

"C'mon, you're blocking traffic." Teresa waved her friend forward.

"Okay. I just wanted the record to be clear."

"Then fill me in on all the juicy details."

"Details?" Shelby asked innocently.

"Don't play coy with me. All of P-town wants to meet the man with the Midas touch. By the way, how rich is he and what does he look like? Answer the second question first."

"Oh, he's your basic tall, dark and . . . not bad-looking."

"Wow! He must be a hunk." Teresa leered theatrically.

"I didn't say that!"

"Oh, yes, you did. You forget, Ms Cool-and-Professional Shelby Haynes, that I know you."

"Well," Shelby said, somewhat peevishly, "I wouldn't want to sound *too* cool and professional, not to mention cynical, but as far as I'm concerned, Captain Lawson is just another... responsibility. I'm not interested in his charm—"

"Ah, charming, too, eh?" Teresa interrupted, to Shelby's annoyance.

"I'm only interested in keeping him and his gang of underwater grave robbers from doing anything to harm the whales who are trying to survive out on Stellwagen Bank."

"Well, amen to that." Teresa grew serious. "But so far he's been a hard man to control. We had Senator Richardson *and* Cape Cod Industries on our side and we couldn't stop his expedition."

"Captain Lawson has very good lawyers," Shelby said sourly, "but if he thinks he'll have it all his own way now, he's in for a surprise. I just finished filing a report citing him for carrying out work without the state-appointed observer—namely me—on board."

*Score one for the baby-sitter.*

"Listen, I'm meeting Tony at the Governor Bradford for a bite of lunch. Care to join us?"

Shelby laughed. "Just what you two need—a fifth wheel. Besides, I have to get home. There's a summer tenant coming in downstairs, and I'm still handling the details for the rental agent. It's annoying, but they take fifty dollars off my rent, so . . ."

"Well, give me a call when you get a chance and fill me in on tall, dark and charming."

"Whose side are you on, anyway?" Shelby laughed. With a wave she turned up her street, climbing the hill until she reached a faded yellow Victorian house.

She took a deep breath of lilac-sweetened air. The purple blossoms cascaded like ripe grapes from the gingerbread trim. During the summer the bottom floor of the house was rented out by the week or month to vacationers, but the upper story, with its panoramic view of Cape Cod Bay, was hers alone to enjoy.

Her nearly antique 1967 Dodge sat parked facing downhill so that when the starter balked, as it did regularly, she could use the incline to push-start it.

She patted the rusting hood absently. "This week, I promise," she murmured under her breath. "I'll get you a brand-new... almost new starter. Really."

As she swung open the front gate, Shelby was nearly bowled over by an energetic bundle of tan fur and floppy ears.

"Cipher!" She play-wrestled her dog to the ground. "Did you miss me? Did you have so much fun barking at all the tourists?"

What was it about a playful dog, she wondered, that brought out the baby talk in otherwise well-adjusted adults?

"C'mon, boy, I'm starving. And I *know* you'll eat."

She watched him bound toward the back stairway, waiting impatiently for her to join him. Last winter, on a particularly solitary Sunday, Shelby had picked Cipher out of the animal shelter, won over by the gangly puppy's doleful eyes and exuberant tail wag. While the shelter attendant could shed no light on the dog's melting pot of a pedigree, he had been adamant about the name, and Cipher clearly recognized it as his own. He was still a bit unruly at times, but what he lacked in the canine etiquette department, he more than compensated for with unequivocal loyalty and a truly first-rate Frisbee catch.

Once inside, after measuring dog food into Cipher's dish and preparing herself a cold turkey sandwich, Shelby headed into her comfortable living room. The apartment boasted a separate dining room, but the impressive mahogany table she'd inherited from her great-aunt always seemed a little forbidding for one person eating alone.

Passing the phone, she noticed the beckoning green light of her answering machine. Two quick blinks: two messages.

Lately she had come to hate that machine. Whenever someone had bad news, it seemed, her little blinking box was there to pass it along. Word of the last two whale fatalities had been delivered in depressing, awkward little messages, punctuated by an annoying beep.

But today was apparently a day for relatively good news. Her first message was from a colleague at the New England Aquarium in Boston: the beached humpback calf they'd picked up a week earlier was making a good recovery and was now expected to survive.

Technically the second message was also good news. Still, it elicited a long groan of protest. Senator Richardson's office was calling to invite Shelby to a dinner party at his home on Nantucket later in the month; they would handle all the arrangements for her flight to the island if she could make it.

She really wasn't in the mood to traipse off and play resident ecology nut for the benefit of a politician, even a friendly politician. Why he'd chosen to visit this unwanted "honor" on her, she could only guess. Still, it was undoubtedly something to do with Safeseas, and she couldn't exactly refuse an invitation from a U.S. senator, could she?

Wonderful. She could spend half a week's pay on a new dress to impress the senator.

So much for the starter.

Jake Lawson paused at the intersection in his rental car and quickly consulted the map on the seat beside him. "You can't miss it," the rental agent had assured him that morning, but he hadn't bargained on the chaotic Sunday tourist traffic that jammed the narrow streets.

He turned left and proceeded down a poorly paved street lined with an assortment of trendy shops and guest houses. He'd spent a good part of the morning trying to line up a rental apartment, but it had been, as it turned out, a useful expenditure of time. He'd narrowed a list of available units down to three when a notation beside one of them caught his eye. He pointed it out to the rental agent.

"Oh, that's the young lady who keeps an eye on the building for us. She's a year-round tenant in the upstairs," the woman said with a smile.

"S. Haynes," he read the name aloud. "That wouldn't be Shelby Haynes?"

"Do you know her? She's such a sweet person."

"Is she?" Jake smiled wryly. "Well, then, I guess that's the place for me."

He found the steep side street at last and pulled to a stop behind a battered wreck of a vehicle with a bumper sticker that said Save the Whales.

"This," he muttered, "must be the place."

He emerged from his car and retrieved a small leather suitcase and a brown paper sack from the trunk, then headed for the broad screened-in porch that would be the entrance to his apartment.

Jake figured he'd already spent far too many nights cramming his big frame into the two-foot-wide berth aboard his vessel, getting up in the dark only to bang his head against the low ceiling. His normally spacious cabin had been sacrificed as a storage area for some of the endless supply of equipment that threatened to swamp the *Questor*.

He had assigned crew members, alternating shifts, to stay aboard the boat at night, and had made arrangements for the rest of his crew at a local hotel.

But he hated hotels. Always had. Soap bars the size of ticket stubs, cardboard mattresses, those idiotic "sanitized" strips on all the toilets: it all made him feel isolated and vaguely depressed. Whenever he could, he opted for more homey accommodations while traveling. Country inns, bed and breakfasts, rented villas—it really didn't matter. Besides, although his crew was almost like a family, they needed the chance to be away from him at the end of the day, to unwind and complain about "the old man."

Thirty-five years old and he was "the old man." He laughed out loud, recalling the first time he had overheard Thomas referring to him that way. You could be nineteen, but if you were the captain, then you were "the old man."

He entered the porch and tested his key in the front door. Inside it was just as he'd expected: airy, cheerful, filled with an assortment of not-quite-antiques. Fresh wildflowers graced the walnut mantel. Jake felt at home the moment he entered the room.

He set down the suitcase and bag and slumped gratefully into a big, overstuffed chair. The rental agent had promised not to give Shelby the name of her new neighbor—an oversight that had cost Jake a crisp twenty-dollar bill. For the life of him, he couldn't explain this growing fascination with the willowy mermaid he'd plucked from the sea only the day before. Overwork? Sunstroke? A touch of the flu? It wasn't like him to play these kinds of games.

A sudden recollection of Shelby burned through him, sucking away his breath like a punch to the belly. She'd been sitting on a deck chair as he'd helped her with that damned wet suit when by accident—it really *had* been an accident—his fingers had grazed that perfect, cool, silken thigh firmed with the muscles of a well-toned athlete. When he'd met her eyes, they were the very gray of the Atlantic in November, filled with the promise of sudden tempests. And unexpectedly, he'd wanted that woman, that virtual stranger, with an urgency he'd never dreamed possible.

Jake tried vainly to shake off the memory, but her image would not disappear.

"Incredible," he muttered under his breath. For months he had lived and breathed only one woman's name: Evangeline. Nothing, and no one, had intruded on that single-minded fixation. Yet now, the merest memory of a woman he scarcely knew and...

This was lunacy, his coming here. Dwelling in the enemy camp, as it were. He was not, to put it mildly, on her list of favorite people at the moment. Odds were she'd have him evicted by nightfall.

Well, he would just have to break it to the lady gently.

From the brown paper sack he withdrew a bottle of Dom Perignon. In all of Provincetown he hadn't been able to find one already chilled, but no matter. He would place it in the freezer and take a leisurely shower.

Then, summoning all his charm, he would say hello to his new neighbor.

SHELBY PULLED AN ARMFUL of fluffy blue towels from her dryer and dropped them into a wicker laundry basket.

"Let's see," she murmured distractedly as she began folding a hand towel into a neat rectangle, "pilot light, fridge on, flowers, sheets and towels... Guess that's everything." One more trip downstairs to unload towels and make up the antique four-poster bed, and she'd be free to reward herself with an afternoon of shopping. If she was going to be on the *Questor* every day, she could use an extra bathing suit. Something... conservative.

When all the towels were folded, she added a set of sheets to the pile and gathered it into her arms. Descending the steep, dimly lit interior staircase that connected the two apartments, she arrived at a door leading to the downstairs pantry. Once inside she checked to ensure that everything in the spacious kitchen was in order. The sound of running water made her pause until she remembered she'd started another load of washing upstairs.

The hallway that led to the main bedroom was dark and quiet, but the bedroom itself was dappled with sunlight filtered by a small oak tree outside the bay window. Shelby dropped her load of sheets and towels onto a cherry sewing rocker in the corner of the room and began to sort through the linens.

She removed a fitted sheet from the pile and unfurled it over the mattress, absently humming an uncertain tune. As she smoothed the sheet into place, leaning over the bed, a prickling sensation needled the back of her neck. She knew at once, even before she straightened, that she was not alone in the room.

As she spun toward the door, a grunted expletive and the distinct splat of wet feet on the polished hardwood floor met her ears. She registered a blur of darkly tanned flesh bisected by a band of white before the bathroom door across the hall slammed shut with such force the entire house seemed to shudder.

Standing alone in the bedroom, sheet clutched to her breast, only the damp footprints on the floor and the fragrance of an herbal shampoo that still hung in the air convinced her she wasn't hallucinating.

The new tenant! Oh, how mortifying! Her face warming with color, she stepped tentatively into the hallway and listened. It was anybody's guess which of them would be more embarrassed. Briefly Shelby entertained the idea of sneaking back up the stairway and pretending the whole awkward encounter had never occurred.

No, that was absurd. These things happened. And they were, after all, two mature adults.

She hoped.

Softly she tapped on the bathroom door. "I, uh, I'm so sorry to have startled you," she stammered. "I wasn't expecting you to arrive till later today."

Silence. He probably felt as awkward as she did, if that was possible.

It was time to beat a hasty retreat. "Well, if you need anything, I'll be right upstairs."

The door opened a few strategic inches, and a damp muscular arm was extended into the hallway.

"For openers, ma'am," came a deep voice tinged with laughter, "I could really use one of those towels. That is, unless you think it's unnecessary."

"You!" Shelby erupted in fury, instantly recognizing the voice. "It's you! You aren't making my life miserable enough? What do you think you're doing in this bathroom?"

To her shock, the door swooped open. Shelby let out a sharp gasp as her hand flew to her mouth.

Before her stood a very damp Jake Lawson, nude from the waist up, his right hand snapping a pair of dangerously low-slung Levi's into place. Amused ebony eyes registered her response.

"You were expecting something more formal?" he inquired suggestively.

Shelby managed a thready exhalation. "Actually I was afraid of something . . . less," she blurted out, momentarily derailed. Her gaze loitered past glistening pectorals to the provocative boundary where faded denim met sun-darkened abdomen.

"That could easily be arranged," he drawled, leaning insolently against the door frame, thumbs hooked in his belt loops.

She jerked her gaze away, ignoring the hard insistent throbbing in her chest. "I'd be fascinated to hear just what you think you're doing here, Captain Lawson."

"Jake. Please."

"I can think of several things to call you, but Jake, most assuredly, is not a top contender."

"Look. I'd planned to break this to you in a less—" he cleared his throat, and briefly lowered his gaze to the floor "—ah, intimate fashion. I really do own a shirt."

She stood her ground in the hallway, refusing to return his rather endearing self-deprecating grin.

"Thing is, we got off to such a rocky start yesterday—"

"Rocky!" Shelby exploded. "You have a real gift for understatement, Captain Lawson. I've already filed the paperwork on your little escapade with the cable. You had no right to be in those waters without me present."

Jake tensed visibly, the cords in his neck tightening. "Nothing we were doing yesterday violated my agreement with the state board, and you know it. I was just testing a magnetometer—a small metal detector. Though I must say I'm impressed with your efficiency."

She ignored the sarcastic bite in his tone. "If you endangered me, you might have endangered a whale."

"In my experience, whales have the sense to watch where they're going."

"I *beg* your par—"

"Fortunately, from now on I'll have you on board, just in case, right?" The tension around his jaw had softened, and his voice was soothing, conciliatory. He sighed, shaking his head. Tiny beads of moisture rained from his wet black curls. "You know," he added quietly, "this isn't at all what

I had in mind when I saw your name on the rental agent's list this morning."

"Oh?"

"I just thought, since we're going to be working together and all—"

"That's about all the togetherness I think I can stand for one lifetime."

Jake chuckled dryly. "But I'm really the perfect neighbor. I don't play loud music . . . often. I won't borrow cups of sugar or power tools and forget to return them, and best of all, I'm hardly ever home, except to sleep."

When he smiled, a tiny dimple appeared in one cheek. For a moment she actually felt herself weakening. After all, it really wasn't her place to object; she was just another tenant, and she didn't want to make trouble with their mutual landlord. And standing here in this steamy bathroom, Jake did seem rather charming.

Suddenly a troublesome thought yanked her back to reality.

"No, no, no." She shook her head adamantly. "Do you realize how this would look? You, living under the same roof as the very person assigned to keep you in line?"

"But a roof is *all* we'd be sharing."

"That's not the point. It's completely out of the question, Captain—Jake. My credibility's at stake."

"Let me get this straight. You're telling me that having me as a neighbor would cause you to compromise your integrity as a scientist?"

"No, of course not. It's just—"

"Then I'm correct in assuming," Jake pursued with all the intensity of a prosecuting attorney, "that you intend to make the next few weeks of my life a living hell, whether or not we're sleeping under the same roof?"

She laughed in spite of herself. "That's a little strong, perhaps, but you've got the general idea."

"It seems to me you're going to have a tough time getting the landlord to break this rental agreement." He withdrew a folded piece of paper from the back pocket of his jeans and presented it to her with an exaggerated flourish. "I've got lawyers who could keep this thing tied up in litigation for years."

Shelby returned the lease to him with an Arctic smile. "No doubt you do. But I'm the only one in all New England who can operate the water heater in the basement. And you don't strike me as the cold shower type."

"I wasn't till I met you."

She was getting nowhere fast. The best thing she could do was terminate the conversation quickly.

Turning to depart, she made an offer. "I'll make some calls upstairs for you. This isn't exactly the only place in town, you know."

"No," he agreed, "but it's certainly the most tempting."

She felt him following closely in the darkened hallway and quickened her steps.

"Too bad," she heard him remark. "Such a fascinating woman, and you're so afraid of what the rest of the world might think."

That wasn't it at all.

She whirled to face him, but he was right on her heels. They collided softly, bodies meeting in an awkward dance.

Strong arms encircled her as they had in the water, buoying, protecting, drawing her in. For the briefest moment only pure, undiluted sensation registered in her mind: her flushed cheek resting on the marble-cool smoothness of his shoulder; a trace of after-shave, exotically spicy; callused fingertips combing back the hair at her temple.

She backed away toward the comforting solidity of the wall, but he stayed with her, gripping her shoulders with proprietary firmness.

"What is it," he whispered huskily, "that makes you so afraid of me?"

She swallowed. "Why on earth would I be afraid of you?"

"You tell me."

She had completely forgotten how to breathe. The man was inciting a delicious rebellion in her body, just touching her shoulders. Since when were shoulders an erogenous zone?

"What was the question?" she asked, stalling.

"The question," he repeated, lips so close to hers she could taste the sweet warmth of his breath, "is why such an intelligent, capable, beautiful woman—"

He paused, tracing an index finger slowly along her cheek.

"Yes?" she pursued, ignoring the shrill warning bell jangling in her head like a fire alarm.

He smiled, and she noticed for the first time a gentle fanning of laugh lines near his eyes. They were kind eyes, brimming with unspoken promises.

"Why such a woman is afraid to trust her own instincts?"

Her gaze dropped to the slight, tantalizing cleft in his chin. She had to quell a crazy desire to reach up and run her finger over it.

Instincts? Her instincts told her she was mad. That the worst thing she could do was let this man get any more involved in her life than he already was.

But did she want to admit, to herself as much as to him, that she couldn't handle having him so near? Besides, when had she ever had the sense to turn down a challenge?

"My instincts, Captain Lawson, tell me you're going to be a bothersome neighbor."

His reaction was guarded, appraising. "You're sure?"

"About your staying, yes. For now. But if you think you've gained anything by your little subterfuge..." She laughed, dismissing the possibility. "And I'm not making any promises about the shower temperature."

She slipped gently from his grasp and began heading down the hallway. Lawson watched her curiously, hands on hips, brows raised. "Well, aren't you supposed to show me around the place? Lecture me about defrosting the refrigerator and all that?"

"It's frost free, but I would like to show you one feature of this house. Follow me."

She led him to the kitchen. "These—" she tapped the first riser of the staircase with a toe "—are the stairs leading to my apartment."

"Oh? That's good to—" Jake began, but she cut him off quickly.

"While you're welcome to use everything else in the apartment, you will not go up those stairs. Do we understand each other?"

"Absolutely, ma'am," he answered solemnly.

She was halfway up before Jake added, just loudly enough for her to hear, "But when you decide to come *down* those stairs, I'll be ready."

# 3

THE DAY of reckoning had arrived.

Shelby sat in the launch, bouncing through the heavy chop, her eyes trained on the rather ungraceful silhouette of the *Questor* now looming into view. It was, she reflected uncharitably, a pretty homely affair, as boats went—a hulking, gunmetal-gray eyesore.

She twisted around and offered a guilty smile to the young crewman, J.B., who was manning the outboard engine. He nodded noncommittally and turned his full attention to a paint blister on the seat beside him.

Was it any wonder she was feeling uncharitable? She didn't want to be there, and as far as the *Questor* crew went, the feeling was probably mutual. That morning at 8:00 when she'd arrived at the wharf for the trip to the boat, she'd been surprised to learn Jake was already out at the site; somehow she'd presumed he would play welcoming committee on this, her first official day as watchdog.

Not that she'd expected balloons and brass bands; she knew the crew probably viewed her, at best, as an annoying interloper. Over time she hoped that she could win their trust, and perhaps even bring them to share the love and respect she felt for her endangered charges.

But from Jake she'd expected something more, some kind of professional truce, particularly after the day before. This commute out to the *Questor* would have been the perfect opportunity for her to lay down some guidelines about their working relationship. She'd made an effort to do just that in his apartment, but today, with him fully clothed and less . . . wet, she would have been better prepared—and less distracted. Which probably explained why he'd sent J.B. to play escort. On his own turf, the *Questor*, Lawson could play commander in chief and expect her to buy his performance.

Shelby bristled at the thought. He'd certainly had no qualms about invading *her* turf. And she didn't like being manipulated, which was what their little encounter in his hallway had been all about. Last night she'd run that same scene through her mind a hundred times, always with the same conclusion: Jake wanted her out of his hair and into his bed.

Well, this was one time Jake Lawson had underestimated his opponent.

"Friends of yours?" Shelby started at the sound of J.B.'s voice, breaking her grim reverie. He pointed toward a pair of dolphins keeping pace with them off the port side. They seemed to be racing with the launch, eyeing its human occupants and grinning quizzically.

"We don't get that many dolphins around here," Shelby said. "Watch. In a minute they'll turn on the speed."

Just as the words were out of her mouth, the pair leaped forward, snaking sinuously in and out of the water as they pulled effortlessly past the launch.

"They like to show off." Shelby smiled. "That still wasn't top speed for them."

The outboard engine's roar died down, and Shelby turned to see that they were already drawing alongside the *Questor*. Watching a crewman lower a ladder over the side, her stomach knotted with apprehension. It felt like her first day at a new job. And in a way, that's all it had to be: a job. If Jake Lawson insisted on turning it into something more—

like a test of wills—then at least the trip out had given her time to prepare for him.

She helped J.B. hand her two duffel bags, loaded with scuba gear and equipment for monitoring the whales, up to a small, red-haired crewman who hoisted them onto the deck. When she'd climbed on board, the man introduced himself pleasantly as Thomas and directed her to the bridge.

She found Jake, dressed in cutoffs and a blue work shirt, hovering over a computer monitor screen. Pale green-and-white printout paper spilled onto the floor from a chattering printer. In strange contrast to the modern technology, an assortment of ancient, worm-riddled tomes was scattered here and there, contributing to an air of controlled chaos.

"Good morning," Shelby ventured in what she hoped was a coolly professional tone. "Or should I say good morning, *Captain*?"

He turned to face her, his gaze skeptical and appraising. "Welcome aboard," he said dispassionately, reaching for her hand. His fingers closed around hers tightly, unwilling to let go. "As a civilian, you're entitled to call me Jake. But then, I thought we'd already cleared that up yesterday."

She chose to ignore the reference, wresting her hand from his warm grasp. "I trust you're all settled?"

"As I ever get. It's a nice place, though I must confess—" he arched an eyebrow "—I had my doubts about the shower temperature this morning."

"Let's just say you're on probation."

"And how long does that last, generally speaking?"

"In your case, indefinitely."

He chuckled good-naturedly. "So," he said, leaning back against the crowded table where the printer churned away, "any trouble connecting with J.B.? I'm sorry I wasn't there to escort you in this morning, but I wanted to get some preliminaries out of the way." He intercepted her wary glance. "Nothing that required your presence. Strictly paperwork—I promise."

Shelby scanned his face suspiciously. Was he testing her already? If so, she'd know soon enough. She smiled frostily. "Why don't you give me a rundown on your plan of attack?"

"You're referring to the treasure hunt, I suppose?" he inquired, giving her a raking glance that left her feeling underdressed in her formfitting jeans and tank top.

She sighed, very loudly. "You suppose correctly."

"Well, let's see. Where should I begin?" His smile faded, and she wondered if her reproof might have had the desired effect. "To start with, we'll be dragging a 'boomer' around for a while. Bottom-penetrating sonar. It sends sound pulses down through the sand till they're reflected back—"

"Until they hit a solid object," Shelby interrupted impatiently. "Then the computer will generate an echo-picture. I don't need a lecture on the equipment, thanks just the same."

"Okay," Jake drawled tolerantly. "I forgot you're an expert. Well, we run back and forth in a grid pattern across this area here." He pointed to a marked area on the navigational chart that was taped to the bulkhead. "At the end of the day we'll see what we've turned up. Then the next day we'll go back out and, more than likely, do it all over again. It could take days, weeks, months even, before we get down to business. You may be very bored by the time this little enterprise is through."

"Oh, I'll manage somehow," Shelby assured him, silently praying she was right. "The important thing is that you and the crew understand *my* role in all this. They need to know that my word is law when it comes to a situation where a whale might be threatened." She looked past him out the window at the cloudless sky, knowing her next words were bound to cause trouble. "I think it will be better for all concerned if we establish a clear chain of command right at the outset."

"Oh?" Jake crossed his arms over his chest. "Are you taking nominations, or is this a one-woman mutiny?"

"I only meant—"

"I know just what you meant, Ms Haynes." His smile was not entirely friendly. "But we have a chain of command already in place."

"Oh?"

"That's right, and it goes like this—I'm the captain. You are the captain's guest." He allowed his unyielding expression to soften into a smile. "And now, like a good host, I'd like to show you around my boat." He glanced at the terminal one last time and hooked a thumb toward the deck below. "C'mon," he said, shepherding her through the door.

Obviously the discussion was closed, as far as Jake was concerned. Fine, Shelby thought, her mouth set in a determined grimace. Time—and the state—were on her side. She and Jake would lock horns soon enough.

She paused as they reached the deck, turning to face him. "Just remember. I'll have my eye on you."

"That's what I'm hoping."

They eased past several large crates as Jake led her back toward the stern. "By the way," he whispered conspiratorially, "I've already told the crew to be on their best behavior."

"How very thoughtful," Shelby muttered. As though she weren't uncomfortable enough!

They paused next to two crewmen who stood hunched over the open engine hatch. Through the opening Shelby could see the tangle of steel and hoses that powered the *Questor*.

"How's it look, boys?" Jake asked.

The slightly built redhead who had helped Shelby aboard looked up. His nose was covered with zinc oxide. "Looks good, Captain. We replaced all the plugs."

"Good." Jake nodded. "Thomas, I'd like you to meet Shelby Haynes."

Shelby extended her hand. "Actually we met briefly," Shelby said.

Thomas wiped his hand on his denim cutoffs and shook hers.

"Ms Haynes is with us to make sure we don't run over any whales while we're out here," Jake explained in a deadpan voice. "And this is Greg."

Shelby shook the second man's hand. He was tall and quite thin and, although no older than Jake, was well on his way to losing his hair.

"I've known Greg for years," Jake went on breezily, "and I've never known him to run down any of your major marine mammals. Thomas, on the other hand, loves his engines and is devoted to reckless speed."

Thomas blushed. "Don't pay any attention to him, Miss Haynes."

"Shelby, please." She smiled.

Jake laughed and patted Thomas's shoulder. "Actually he throws a tantrum if I go over ten knots."

Jake moved on toward the cabin with Shelby at his heels. Inside they found the older crewman she remembered from her ill-fated first encounter with the *Questor*, rummaging in a toolbox and whistling softly to himself.

"Shelby Haynes, Marcus Sears. Marcus is about the closest thing we have to a real sailor on board," Lawson announced. "Merchant marine, mate on a tugboat, fisher-man...."

"My best friend's father is a fisherman," Shelby offered. "His name's Cabral. Do you know him?"

"No," Marcus said shortly. "I worked out of Bedford, not here."

"Oh. Well, nice to meet you," Shelby said, nonplussed.

"You seen the needle-nosed pliers, Captain?" Marcus asked.

"Check Thomas. You know how he is with tools."

His hand at the small of her back, Jake directed Shelby out of the cabin and back out on deck. "Don't mind Marcus," he told her once they were safely out of earshot. "Small talk's not his strong point."

"I gathered that."

Jake laughed. "He's a damn fine sailor, though." They strolled toward the bow, Jake pausing every so often to clear their path or check out a piece of equipment. "All my people are first-rate. I've been very lucky. Except, of course—" he raised his voice with a wink "—for J.B. over there. He's been a troublemaker since the day we met."

J.B., who was prying open a wooden crate near the bow, laughed loudly. "Takes one to know one, sir." He set aside his crowbar and tilted back his baseball cap, barely reining in a headful of rebellious brown curls.

"How did you two get together, anyway?" Shelby asked, more out of politeness than real curiosity.

"Well, it's a little embarrassing, Miss Haynes—"

"Call me Shelby."

"Okay, then, if you say so. Shelby." He smiled tentatively. "Anyway, I met the captain down in Fort Lauderdale while I was trying to lift the stereo out of his dashboard."

"You were breaking into his car?" Shelby asked incredulously. J.B. might be in his twenties, but he could easily pass for a teenager. And he had the face of a choirboy.

"Yes, ma'am. Or actually, I'd already broken in by that point." He grinned sheepishly. "You see, I was pretty much of a beach bum there for a while. Surfing and panhandling. Sometimes made a couple of bucks passing out handbills, but to be honest, I was starting to slide over the line, if you know what I mean."

Shelby glanced at Jake, who nodded affirmation.

"So there I was, just got the stereo out of the dashboard and I look up and see this guy sitting on the beach wall shaking his head. He said to me, 'Son, you're awful careful for a thief.' Said a professional thief would have just ripped out the stereo and been long gone, but there I was, trying not to damage the dashboard." J.B. laughed at the memory. "Said I didn't have the mentality of a thief, that I ought to try something where I could put my talents to work and make some real money. Then he asked me what I thought of gambling. Whether I would like to work my butt off for pocket change against the chance of a fortune in sunken treasure."

"Not the sort of offer one gets every day." Shelby smiled.

But J.B.'s voice was serious. "No, ma'am. More like a—" he groped for words "—a lifeline thrown to a drowning man." He was silent for a moment, then suddenly brightened. "Back then, my mom used to cry when I'd call her up . . . usually for money. And now she's living in the house I bought her with my share from our last salvage." He met Jake's eyes, and a look of understanding seemed to pass between them. "So here I am," J.B. concluded, "gambling on the captain again."

Shelby smiled at the young man's enthusiasm. "And just what are the chances, J.B.? Of finding the *Evangeline*, I mean?"

"About a million to one," Jake answered for him. "Care to place a bet?"

"Thanks, no. I'll stick with the lottery. My odds are better." Glancing toward the prow, Shelby noticed both her duffel bags stashed next to a coil of rope. "Oh, there they are," she said absently, mulling over locations where she could safely set up shop while remaining out of harm's way—and the crew's.

"I see you like to travel light," Jake remarked.

"I brought some listening equipment along with my scuba gear. I'd planned to tow a sonobuoy behind us so that I could listen as well as look for the whales."

"Need any help?" J.B. offered.

"Thanks, J.B. Maybe later. The thing is—" she chewed on her bottom lip pensively "—the best place for me would be on the bow, but with the sea this choppy, I'll spend the whole day wiping off my binoculars. I wouldn't accomplish much."

"Beyond a serious case of seasickness, no," Jake agreed. His eyes traveled the deck. "Why not set up on the bridge?" he suggested at last. "You'll have a good view that way, and if I get too reckless, you can stage a mutiny."

J.B. smothered a laugh, studying Shelby carefully for her reaction.

"I'm not sure we'd survive together in confined quarters for an entire day."

"Oh, sure we will. I'm the easiest guy in the world to get along with. Tell her, J.B."

"He's the easiest guy in the world to get along with," J.B. echoed automatically, barely squelching a smile.

"That's what they said about Captain Queeg," Shelby muttered, heading for her duffel bag to retrieve her binoculars and notebook.

"I don't think I've heard of him," J.B. said, his forehead furrowed in thought. "Where's his home port?"

"Back to work, J.B." Jake laughed, shaking his head. "Need a hand, Ms Haynes?"

"This is all I'll need for the time being," Shelby said, following Jake reluctantly back to the bridge. She had serious reservations about spending the day in such close proximity, but there didn't seem to be much choice.

"Are you sure I won't be in the way?" she asked as they made their way up a steep set of metal stairs.

"Oh, you'll be in the way, all right—but then, you'll be in the way no matter where you are."

She didn't respond, and when they reached the bridge, he paused just inside and touched her shoulder. "Hey," he said, his voice gentled, "I'm sorry. It was just a joke."

"You know, you're not making this any easier for me," she blurted out angrily.

"Really?" Jake asked in all seriousness, motioning her toward a deck chair in the corner. "Believe it or not, I thought I was."

"By ridiculing me in front of your crew? By—"

"Hey," Jake broke in. "Lighten up a little, will you? I was just trying, in my own clumsy, good-ol'-boy way—" he acknowledged her groan with a smile "—to inject a note of humor into a tense situation. Obviously it backfired on me." He laughed wryly. "Wouldn't be the first time."

Shelby cleared a pile of aging, mildewed maps off the deck chair and sat down. Things were not going well, and she'd been on board the *Questor* less than an hour. It did not bode well for the future. It did not even bode well for the day.

Jake positioned himself on the edge of a chart-strewn table next to her. "I guess this is hard on you, huh? Stuck here in this loony bin when you could be back at Safeseas? I imagine those folks really miss you."

"Some of them are actually jealous," Shelby told him, skeptical of his newly conciliatory tone. "For some bizarre reason this is considered glamorous work." She rolled her eyes derisively. "A plum assignment."

"Well, I'm sure you'll put them straight on that score right quick. Treasure hunting is anything but glamorous."

"That all depends on the result. J.B sounded like a convert."

Jake shrugged. "Not all hunts have such happy endings. As it happens, the *Saragossa* salvage did."

The name rang a vague bell. "I think I remember reading about that," Shelby told him. "Down near some island a couple of years back?"

"Antigua." Jake nodded. "A Spanish galleon, relatively intact." He smiled, almost wistfully. "A real dream find. They're still cataloging some of the artifacts we uncovered."

"And the take?" Shelby prompted skeptically.

"Two million in bullion, give or take. Course, that's small change compared to what's on board the *Evangeline*."

"I understood that the *Evangeline* was at least half-legendary. For all we know, you could be on a very expensive wild-goose chase."

His smile told her he'd heard it all before. "If you look hard enough, you can find a grain of truth in almost every legend."

"That'd better be one impressive grain to make you gamble all this." Shelby waved her arm toward the deck.

"Oh, it is." Jake nodded slowly. "It definitely is."

Shelby watched him curiously as he walked over to a small metal safe in the corner.

"Of course, a lot of detective work preceded this," he said, twisting the dial on the safe as he spoke. "I'd been collecting data on the *Evangeline* for six years—newspapers, diaries, somebody's great-great-great-uncle who remembered hearing tales about the pirate ship that sank off the Cape.... I hit a lot of dead ends before I came up with this."

He reached into the safe and retrieved a black, leatherbound book of some kind, the gold leaf filigree around its edges nearly worn away by use. "This," Jake explained, returning to Shelby and presenting the book to her, "is the log of the *Evangeline*'s captain."

Shelby took the slim volume from his hands carefully. Thumbing through the pages, worn thin as rice paper, she saw a beautiful, almost feminine script.

"I located it through a book dealer, who bought it at an estate auction up in Maine. The ship's mate carried it to shore—he was one of the few who survived the hurricane that night—and a week later he was hung as a pirate for his pains."

"How fascinating," Shelby murmured, genuinely intrigued. "I'll bet it makes for juicy reading."

"They were a rowdy bunch, the *Evangeline* crew," Jake agreed, his tone almost reverential. "And that log is the reason I've been able to narrow my search down to this little patch of Stellwagen Bank."

The name jarred Shelby back to reality. "Speaking of Stellwagen," she said, returning the log to Jake, "hadn't you better get going? I get the feeling I'm keeping you from your work."

"You really are all business, aren't you?" Jake remarked as he carried the log back to his safe. "Don't you know all work and no play makes Jill a dull girl?"

Shelby pulled out her binoculars and began cleaning the lenses with a furious attention to detail. If she ignored Jake now, maybe she could set the tone for the future; there was no point in letting him goad her.

"Raise anchor!" Jake called down to the crew, and within a few minutes the boat was picking up steam, its huge engines making the deck vibrate under their feet.

Shelby lifted the binoculars to her eyes and began a careful survey of the water, but except for a spout about a quarter of a mile off starboard, there was no sign of whales on the white-capped sea. Even with the boat now moving, the morning sun had raised the temperature on the bridge, and she fashioned a makeshift fan out of a newspaper to keep herself cool.

Jake stood casually, one arm draped on the big teak wheel, while he focused most of his attention on the computer monitor.

"So," he continued their conversation where he'd left off, "what do you do for play?" He glanced over his shoulder at Shelby. "Seen any good movies lately?"

Obviously this was not a man who liked to work in silence. "Actually," Shelby answered evenly, "I don't go to movies in the summer. The nearest theater's in Wellfleet, and with all the tourists, the lines get so long..." She shrugged, hoping she'd made things clear. She intended to keep her distance.

"I hear there are some great restaurants in P-town," Lawson went on, undeterred. "Any recommendations?"

"Oh, there are some fine seafood places," Shelby agreed. "Thing is, the tourists pretty much mob them, and you can never get a decent table. When you get right down to it, I don't eat out much in the summer."

"I see." Lawson pursed his lips. "I think I sense a pattern developing here. How about concerts?"

"There're some nice candlelight chamber concerts in Truro," Shelby said, still staring through her binoculars. "Of course, in the summer getting hold of tickets can be a problem, what with the—"

"Tourists." Jake shook his head resignedly. "No wonder Jill's a dull girl," he commented under his breath. "She never gets out of the house."

Shelby, cooling herself with her fan, smiled behind the newspaper. At least, she thought, she'd made her point.

"I apologize for the heat," Jake told her, at last changing the subject. "It can get pretty miserable up here some-times—at least, that's what I keep telling the crew. But I'm afraid that old parchment and salt spray don't mix."

"It's not so bad. But you'd better find what you're after by August, when it really heats up."

"Fat chance." Jake began unbuttoning his work shirt. "I hope this won't offend you, Ms Haynes, but if we're going to be working together all summer, you might as well get used to the dress code right now." He shrugged off his shirt and tossed it onto a chair.

"It's your boat," Shelby murmured, eyes glued to the sea.

"I'm glad you realize that." Jake returned his attention to the monitor, silent at last.

In the sudden quiet Shelby found she was feeling even more uncomfortable. She allowed herself a surreptitious glance in Jake's direction. He was studying a printout, a fine sheen of sweat making his broad back shimmer in the oblique rays of golden sun.

Deep in her temples she felt the undeniable beginnings of a first-rate headache. Probably the heat, combined with all her tensions about work. And she'd skipped breakfast en-tirely.

"Excuse me . . . uh, Jake . . ."

"Hmm?"

"Do you know where I could find some aspirin?"

"Down in the head, probably. Check the medicine cabinet. Nothing terminal, I hope?"

"A headache that would kill a lesser woman." She set aside her binoculars. "But not to worry. I'm tough."

"Don't get lost."

She made her way below decks and passed through the tiny, stainless-steel galley and on past a wardroom decorated with sagging maps and posters. She could see the way to the head, but another door on her right was wide open. Pausing in the doorway, curious, she saw a small, neat cabin. Bookshelfs lined the walls, each shelf equipped with its own brass guardrail as a precaution against rough weather. It appeared the room was primarily for storage; several large wooden crates took up most of the available space. But on a small oak desk in the corner a familiar white pamphlet caught Shelby's eye, and without thinking, she entered the room to check out her suspicion.

Sure enough, it was a Safeseas leaflet, full of the kind of information they mailed out to new converts or contributors. But what was it doing here, of all places?

She studied the shelf overhead. A small volume with a gold bookmark drew her attention. She twisted around as a twinge of guilt came over her. Whoever the cabin belonged to, she definitely did not belong in it. Still, the bookmark beckoned. She lifted the book off the rack, and her mouth dropped open as she came to a dog-eared page. "Sonnets?" she whispered incredulously. Shakespeare was not exactly the kind of light reading one might have expected of the crew.

She replaced the volume and noticed a stack of CDs piled on top of a small compact disc player. Pulling down the topmost CD, she examined the plastic cover.

"Yuck," she murmured. "Great Country-Western Hits of Yesterday."

"To each his own."

She whirled to find Jake leaning in the tiny doorway.

"I, uh . . ."

"Mistook this for the head?" Jake suggested. "I was afraid you got lost."

"Oh, Lord, this is so embarrassing." She put her hand to her cheek and felt it blazing. "I just saw the Safeseas pamphlet, and naturally I was wondering why anyone here would have it."

" 'Know thine enemy' is the phrase, I think." He reached for her hand. "I like to know what I'm up against," Jake said softly. "Apparently so do you."

She moved toward the door, but he blocked her path, overwhelming the tiny room by his presence. He still held her hand in a grip gentle enough to allow an escape that she did not seek, and when he lowered his head to meet her lips so suddenly and inexplicably, she felt herself respond automatically—eyes closed, head tilted back, hand reaching for his shoulder to pull him to her—

Instead, at the last minute she pushed him away.

"What am I doing?" she wondered aloud, breathless with alarm. "What am I doing?"

"Knowing thine enemy?" Jake ventured with a sly smile.

"You have to understand," Shelby insisted, her gaze locking on his, "I don't want this. Really I don't."

"Look," Jake reassured her kindly. "Nothing happened, okay? It's my fault, anyway, and I promise to behave myself from here on out. Deal?"

Shelby exhaled shakily. "Deal."

"Besides—" Jake winked "—I knew you had a headache."

A sudden loud cry interrupted their laughter.

"Fire!" a voice screamed. "Damn it, get the fire extinguisher, somebody!"

"Captain!" came an urgent plea.

Jake was sprinting through the galley and up the stairs before Shelby could even react. She followed him onto the deck toward the upstairs cabin, where an ominous trail of smoke spiraled from the doorway. She raced to join the other crew members huddled anxiously by the stern.

"Outta the way!" she heard Jake rasp. Greg and Marcus emerged, choking and sputtering. Shelby watched in silence, her throat constricted by a potent combination of smoke and fear, as Jake disappeared into the cabin.

They heard the loud whoosh of a fire extinguisher as a powdery white haze churned from the doorway. At last, after what seemed ages, Jake emerged from the seething cloud, his face streaked with soot, his brow dripping.

"Okay, everybody," he said, forcing lightness into his smoke-raw voice, "who's been playing with matches?"

The crew emitted a collective, relieved laugh.

"By the time we found it, it seemed like half the cabin was burning," Greg explained.

"What's the damage, Captain?" Marcus asked.

"Could've been worse." Jake settled on a wooden crate, wiping his brow with his sleeve. "Not much damage to the bulkheads, but we lost a lot of charts and maps." He paused, perusing their expectant, anxious faces. "Not to worry. I have duplicates, of course."

"So," Marcus pursued, "do we pack it in for the day?"

Jake managed a grin, his clenched jaw accentuating the stern lines of his profile. "Hell, no. We don't pack it in. This is just a minor annoyance, nothing more, nothing less. Marcus, get whoever else isn't busy right now and start cleaning this mess up. Greg, check that sonar cable." He paused for effect, careful not to single anyone out with his eyes. "I'm not going to ask who screwed up and left a cigarette burning, or whatever else may have started that fire, but I do want to remind you all that we are a long way from shore and are carrying a couple of hundred gallons of gasoline in our tanks. I can think of better places to get careless with fire." He waited to let the message sink in, as his crew stood silent. "All right," he said, breaking the spell at last. "Back to work. I'm not paying you minimum wage to stand around and work on your tans."

Again the sheepish, relieved laughter, the release of tension. Shelby had to admit he had a talent for defusing a tough situation and rallying his people.

But when Jake rejoined her after inspecting the damaged cabin, his face was unnaturally drawn.

"How are you doing?" Shelby asked.

Jake roused himself from his brooding reverie. "Oh, I'm none the worse for wear. But I'll tell you, this has got to let up soon. We've had a string of bad luck you wouldn't believe." He stroked his mustache pensively.

"Such as?"

"Well, the usual delays you write into the script for this kind of exploration. Weather, permits and such—that I expect. But in the past week since we got here, we've had engine trouble, the depth finder's gone out twice and the radar is still on the blink. I can't figure it out. It's mostly new, state-of-the-art equipment. Guess we're just having an unlucky streak."

"And I'm a part of that unlucky streak, I assume?" Shelby inquired lightly.

"No," Jake answered slowly, pensively. "I've got a strange feeling you may just change my luck for the better."

# 4

WHILE JAKE AND THE CREW were busy cleaning up the aftermath of the fire, Shelby moved her gear off the bridge and down onto the bow. The sea was only slightly calmer, but even if it meant getting wet, it would be safer all around for her to stay off the bridge.

She'd just finished settling in when she looked up to see the only woman crew member heading toward her. The small, slim woman, her chestnut hair sleeked back in a casual ponytail, was carrying a paper plate and a mug of cold milk.

"Here you go," she said, handing the plate to Shelby. "Emergency rations. I'm Janine, by the way. We haven't been officially introduced."

"Shelby Haynes." Shelby took the milk and plate awkwardly in one hand and shook hands with the other. She turned her attention to the sandwich and smiled. "Peanut butter and jelly?"

"Actually it's a purée of toasted peanuts served al dente."

"In other words, chunky?"

"Exactly." Janine winked. "With the saltiness of the peanuts perfectly complemented by the tart sweetness of a *conserve de framboise*."

"Raspberry. My favorite." Shelby laughed.

"I could go on," Janine offered.

"No really. You'll have me thinking I should have dressed up for lunch."

"Well, it's a shame, really," Janine said. "I had a great meal planned, but the fire left a coat of ashes all over the galley." She lowered her voice confidentially. "You realize there's a war on over who's the best cook?"

"You're kidding."

"I wouldn't kid about that. First it was the captain, doing his Texas barbecue recipe with shrimp, and then Marcus has to top him with a bouillabaisse he whipped up in about twenty minutes. Which," she added in an aside, "is practically cheating, since he was a professional cook in the merchant marine for years. Then my own fiancé comes up with Veal Picatta—"

"Your fiancé?" Shelby asked, puzzled.

"Greg." Janine looked at her quizzically. "Didn't you know about us? Well, of course not. Why should you? I asked him to the Sadie Hawkins dance our freshman year in high school, and we've been together ever since." She gave an embarrassed shrug. "Corny, huh?"

"Corny," Shelby agreed, "but sweet."

"Anyway, in the galley war, as we're calling it, I think my honey has the lead for now. But never fear—Janine Gendron has not met the man she can't beat in a duel with saucepans." A look of dark suspicion creased her brow. "Wait a minute," she challenged, "what about you?"

Shelby laughed ruefully. "Believe me, I'm no threat. In my hands a microwave oven's a lethal weapon. But, hey, you haven't mentioned J.B. and Thomas's contributions."

"Actually, when my fish was ruined, they volunteered to help. You're eating their contribution."

LUNCH WAS SCARCELY DONE when Shelby felt the engines die and looked up in surprise from her bored, almost trance-like survey of the waves. She watched curiously as Marcus dropped anchor and Greg and J.B. stripped off their shirts and jumped off the stern into the water.

"What's going on?" she called to Jake as he approached.

"We're going to dig," he explained, his voice excited. "There's not much to go on, but we've had some interesting readings here, and it's a chance to test the equipment. Frankly, since our little close call with incineration this morning, everyone's been moping around looking depressed. They could use a break in the tedium. And after all—" he touched her lightly on the shoulder, and a little thrill shimmered through her belly "—I've got you here for luck."

Shelby followed Jake to the stern railing and bent over to see the two crewmen dive down to the area where the propellers were located, surface to catch their breath, then dive again.

"We call these 'mailboxes,'" Jake explained, as two elbow-shaped tubes were secured over the propellers. "We turn on the engines, and voilà, you have one serious blender."

"Very ingenious," Shelby remarked, watching as Jake checked with his divers. When he was reassured and the men were safely back aboard, he turned and cupped his hands around his mouth.

"All right, Janine," he yelled, "let her rip."

Shelby listened as the engines throbbed back to life, and the *Questor*'s powerful screws forced water down the tubes to the seafloor below.

"Another half hour and we'll have a crater twelve feet deep and three times as wide," Jake called over the groaning engines. "It's messy, but very effective."

"I'll need to get an underwater view of those things at work," Shelby mused.

"I'm afraid you wouldn't see much. It would just look like a big underwater sandstorm. Besides, it could be dangerous."

"Dangerous?" Shelby inquired sharply. "And what about the sea life in the area?"

"I'm sure it's no problem," Jake hastened to reassure her. "The fish have the sense to get out of the way. Only human beings are dumb enough to go looking for trouble."

"Meaning?"

"Meaning nothing." Jake held up his hands, his eyes rolled heavenward in a show of exasperation. "Just a joke."

"Well, it won't be a joke to the animals whose habitats you are preparing to . . . to put through a blender." Damn the man. He was going to take this seriously, like it or not!

Anger was tightening Jake's jaw. He started to speak but bit back his words, reconsidering. "Let me be up-front with you on this, Ms Haynes," he finally said, loading her name with unconcealed sarcasm. "Sooner or later, I'm going to dig, and when I do, there may be one or two unhappy crabs or sea urchins forced to relocate. That's inevitable. Unfortunate, but inevitable. *Your* job is to look after the whales—"

"My job," Shelby interrupted icily, "is defined by the state board that assigned me to protect the marine environment here. I'm sure I don't have to remind you, Captain Lawson," she returned his sarcasm, "that you agreed, in writing, that my decision will be final. But—" she held up a hand, shutting off Jake's angry retort "—I am a reasonable woman. My decision is that you may proceed—for now. I will go down and inspect the site after you have . . . puréed it, and assess the degree of harm."

Jake hunched his formidable shoulders forward and glowered down at her menacingly. Shelby stood her ground, meeting his gaze unflinchingly.

"You know," he said at last, turning toward the bridge, "you're beautiful, even when you're being unreasonable. Still, I wonder if I shouldn't save myself a lot of grief by just tying you to the anchor and throwing you overboard now."

He didn't wait to hear her answer, which was probably just as well.

WITHIN AN HOUR Shelby found herself submerged in the chilly Atlantic, following Jake, Greg and Thomas toward the ocean floor, where the mailboxes had created what looked like a moon crater. She paced herself, staying a few feet back to keep them within sight, her focus inevitably returning to Jake's muscular, blue-suited form.

To her amusement, each diver was equipped with a pair of ordinary Ping-Pong paddles to dig at the bottom and fan away loosened sand. They proved to be wonderfully efficient. The divers worked diligently while she surveyed the area. It was almost barren sand, and she had to admit her worries had been unfounded. Still, it had been a good opportunity to put Jake on notice.

Hovering a few feet above the ocean floor, she divided her attention between watching him work—it really *was* work, after all—and keeping an eye on the bluefin tuna who was watching the excavation with an expression of surprised disapproval.

At last Jake signaled that it was time to return to the boat. The mailboxes had served their morale-boosting purpose, whether or not they had hit pay dirt.

A bit disappointed, in spite of the fact that, officially at least, she cared nothing about the treasure, Shelby prepared to follow. Jake and the others were already several feet above her, outlined against the gloomy light. She coiled her legs beneath her and kicked off from a mound of freshly disturbed sand, but the sand gave way, and she achieved very little momentum.

Suddenly she realized that her heel had struck something hard and sharp edged. With only a moment's hesitation she doubled back and dug her gloved hand into the dirt until she found the object. Freeing it from the sand, she could feel that it was rectangular, its sides too flat, the angles too precise to have been fashioned by nature. Barely able to contain her excitement, she sped upward until she pulled alongside Jake.

He took the object, nodded and patted her happily on the back.

The slow trip back up to the surface seemed endless. When they had reached the bobbing stern of the boat, Jake pulled back his face mask and released his mouthpiece.

"Snuffbox," he told Shelby and his two crewmen floating close at hand. "Gold." He scraped away the sediment covering it, rinsing the box in the water, until it gleamed in the sunlight.

"It's engraved! If I can only..." He dug furiously at it with his fingernails, holding it up for closer inspection, until an incandescent smile lit up his face.

"W.S.C.!" he shouted, loud enough for the crew on board the boat to hear. "W, S and C!"

Cheers broke out immediately, and J.B., who was swimming close by, threw his arm around Shelby's neck in a brotherly gesture of affection.

"Who is W.S.C.?" Shelby asked Jake, mystified.

"W.S.C.," Jake repeated happily. "Why, that would be William Seth Curry, unless I miss my guess."

"William—" Shelby began.

"The captain of the *Evangeline*. The one and only One-Arm Willy Curry!" Jake exulted. "I told you you'd bring me luck!"

SHELBY SCOOPED ANOTHER SPOONFUL of Heavenly Hash from the carton on her kitchen table and glanced at the clock on her microwave.

Nine-thirty-five p.m. Five minutes later than the last time she'd checked.

In the apartment below a chorus of voices surged and receded like a windswept sea. The soft evening breeze carried a woman's melodious giggle through Shelby's open window.

A day and a half into his tenancy, and Jake Lawson was having a party.

Guiltily Shelby savored another spoonful of ice cream. One of these days she would have to learn to stop resorting to her freezer in times of emotional stress. Thus far, vigorous exercise had kept the evidence of her sweet tooth off her hips, but how much longer would good genes and jogging come to her aid?

Mentally she computed the toll. A bag of M & Ms and a pint of Heavenly Hash—somewhere in the neighborhood of five trillion calories. Enough to keep her out of the new one-piece bathing suit she had picked up the afternoon before.

And the bathing suit wasn't all she'd purchased. There had been a black lace teddy in the boutique window, a hankie's worth of fabric held together by satin bows and a lot of optimism. For some crazy reason she'd bought it on the spot. Without even trying it on, for crying out loud!

What on earth had possessed her? she wondered, frowning. She had never in her entire life owned anything so...well, provocative, not even during her marriage. Now here she was, buying lingerie that would make a store mannequin blush when the only male who ever set foot in her bedroom was Cipher. And even he preferred the living room.

A burst of male laughter punctuated the air. No doubt Jake was continuing the impromptu festivities begun on his boat that afternoon after her inadvertent discovery of the snuffbox.

"This," Jake had explained to her, "is the validation we've been looking for. We could have dredged up cannonballs and pieces of eight for a year without being absolutely sure we were near the *Evangeline*, but you, my friend, have provided us with a mighty strong link on our very first dig."

Somehow, helping Jake Lawson toward his goal had not been quite what she'd had in mind, and she had declined his casual invitation to drop by downstairs for a drink. She'd assumed he had something more private, and less innocent, in mind. Now, because of her refusal to join in, she probably looked like a snob.

Well, she should have known Jake was the type to throw wild parties. Okay, maybe not wild. Actually, by any reasonable standard the party was tame enough, but the murmur of voices set her teeth on edge nonetheless. Perhaps it reminded her a bit too clearly of her own self-imposed isolation since her divorce,

No, that wasn't entirely the truth. And Shelby tried at all times to be honest—painfully honest—with herself.

The truth was, she had to admit that somewhere along the way she'd lost control of the situation in Jake's apartment the day before. The mere scent of him, the feel of him, had flooded her with raw sensation and left her feeling tingly, vibrant . . . alive. And today in his cabin his careless, callused touch had been enough to short-circuit all her careful programming, and Shelby did not relish the idea of losing control. Not again. And especially not to a man like Jake.

He was a phantom, a perpetual wanderer. She had seen it in his eyes. The kind of man who refused to be claimed, though undoubtedly many women had tried. And he was right beneath her feet at this very moment probably having the same tantalizing effect on some other hapless female who had wandered into his orbit and been swept off her feet. The thought made her vaguely queasy.

"Too much ice cream," she muttered aloud to Cipher. He thumped his tail agreeably in his sleep.

In any case, it would be better all the way around if she kept her distance. Their relationship had to be essentially adversarial in order for her to do her job.

So why did her nerves twitch every time she heard laughter float up from his apartment?

She needed a little fresh air. Her kitchen was becoming downright claustrophobic.

"Come on, Cipher. Let's take a walk," she suggested. The dog responded with a joyous yelp, racing down the stairs to the back lawn as soon as Shelby opened the door.

The breeze was ocean cooled and heavy with honeysuckle. Glowing lights from Jake's apartment lit the lawn, and the milky translucence of a full moon highlighted the leaves of surrounding trees with a lining of silver. Shelby hurried to the shadow of a huge oak that spread its canopy over half the grounds, feeling conspicuous in the brightness. The melancholy strains of some old country ballad drifted from the downstairs windows.

Leaning back against the rough coolness of the tree trunk, she watched as Cipher attempted unsuccessfully to locate the bone he'd buried the previous day. With furious concentration he sniffed the perimeter of the lawn, nose twitching, pendulous ears swaying. Every so often he paused to paw the ground frantically, only to abandon the effort a few seconds later with an embarrassed glance in his mistress's direction.

"I know how he feels," came a deep-timbred male voice from the darkness.

"Jake?"

"Evening," he answered softly, joining her beneath the tree. In the moon's shimmering light his face was a mosaic of bright, chiseled contours and deep, impenetrable shadows. She saw he was carrying an unopened bottle of champagne and two water tumblers.

"I thought you always found what you were looking for." She smiled faintly to soften the barb.

"No," he answered almost wistfully. "Not always." He sat down on the grass, legs crossed Indian-style. "Join me?"

Shelby hesitated for a minute, fabricating feeble rationales for saying no. How much harm could a few minutes of conversation do?

Plenty.

At last she settled next to him, wrapping her gauzy cotton skirt around her knees.

"So what's he after?" Jake whispered, nodding toward the dog.

"Buried treasure." Her voice was edged with more sarcasm than she'd really intended. For some reason his presence here made her feel slightly off balance and defensive.

His lips eased into a smile. "A kindred spirit."

As if to prove the point, Cipher, roused by the unfamiliar male voice, bounded toward him like a long-lost friend, settling most of his furry bulk in Jake's lap.

"Down, boy," Shelby chastised halfheartedly.

"That's okay. We seem to have reached an understanding," Jake studied her face searchingly. "I was hoping you and I might do the same. Hence the wine. Unfortunately I seem to have run out of wineglasses."

"I would have stocked a couple of hundred more if I'd known you were planning on entertaining half the population of the town."

Jake winced. "Pretty loud, huh?"

She sighed. "No, not really. I'm just used to...the quiet." She looked away, avoiding his steady gaze.

"It's just the crew and some of the folks we've met around town. I'll put out the word to cool it." He moved to gently dislodge Cipher from his lap.

"No." Shelby reached impulsively for his wrist. Beneath her fingers she felt a soft dusting of hair and the cool metal of a watchband. "It's all right," she assured him, removing her hand as quickly as she had extended it. "I sort of like the music."

"If you say so." Jake settled back, and she watched as he peeled back the wire cage of the champagne bottle. There was a muted pop, and he poured sparkling wine into the tumblers with practiced ease.

"What about your party?" she ventured, her voice betraying her with an unfamiliar shakiness.

"They'll never miss me." He handed her a glass. "To finding what you're looking for," he offered, glass raised in a toast.

Her breath caught at the husky softness in his tone. She touched his glass with hers, then took a slow sip, wondering at the enigma sitting just inches from her on the grass.

"What makes a man run off and dig for treasure, anyway?" she asked, curiosity overcoming her lingering sense of awkwardness.

He shrugged, scratching Cipher's ear gently, apparently lost in thought. "It pays the bills, I suppose."

"Then if that's all there is to it, why not be a CPA?"

Laughing, he shook his head slowly. "I'm afraid I'm not much of a desk jockey. Tried it in Fort Worth for a few years, though. Real estate, mostly. Then one day I pushed one pencil too many and something just snapped. I booked an evening flight to Barbados and never looked back."

Shelby narrowed her eyes skeptically. "You're telling me you just dropped everything and ran away from home?"

"Yes. In a manner of speaking."

"But didn't you miss your family in Texas?" Shelby pursued. "Weren't you homesick?"

Jake shook his head pensively. "Home," he said at last, "is wherever the *Questor*'s anchored."

There was a wistful note in his voice that was unmistakable. Could it be, Shelby wondered, that the man who had everything was lonely?

"Somehow, when I'm on the water, I don't know...everything makes sense. It's where I belong, the only place I'm really sure of myself. It's strange, when you think about it, for a landlubber from the heart of Texas. I didn't even see an ocean till I was eighteen. My first real love affair was with the sea."

"Don't you mean with what's *under* the sea?" Shelby plucked a dandelion by her feet and twirled it between her fingertips. Something about Jake's words had upset her. Oh, she knew just how he felt: the sea was her lifeblood, after all, but his affection for it didn't jibe with her image of the man. He was the sea's plunderer; she was its protector. Now he was blurring the distinction. He couldn't possibly understand how she felt, could he?

"You know, you have a talent for troublesome questions." Jake grimaced good-naturedly. "What's under the sea gives me an excuse to be on the sea."

"So catch lobsters for a living," she pursued intractably. "Hire on a fishing boat. I know some guys down at the wharf who are always looking for a few good men."

Jake rubbed his jaw thoughtfully. The glint in his dark eyes told her she'd made her point, but he wasn't about to concede it.

"Naw." He smiled knowingly at some private secret. "Then I'm guaranteed to find what I'm looking for. Where's the fun in that?" He refilled their glasses in silence, then added, "Besides, I like the thrill of the chase."

"Thanks for the warning."

"I suppose there's no element of adventure in your job, eh?" He was deliberately baiting her, determined to regain the upper hand. "No thrill of the chase, just dry science and high-mindedness?"

Taken aback, Shelby laughed out loud. "I won't deny there's an element of adventure. But there's also what you call 'dry science.' Even a bit of high-mindedness."

"Like finding the cause of the whales' sickness?"

"I guess so." She paused, self-conscious at the turn the conversation was taking. "Mostly, though, it's just a job. Up until this latest crisis, I'd been collating data on whale songs. To human ears, they're just long, very beautiful melodies, but if we find the key to the language, perhaps we'll actually be able to talk to another species."

"Like breaking a secret code." Jake nodded his head in approval. "What a fascinating mystery."

"I suppose it is, at that."

"And you love pursuing that mystery, don't you? The combination of thorough research, hard work and lucky hunches? A lot like hunting for treasure."

Shelby smiled. "We don't play hunches in my line of work. We formulate theories."

"A gamble, by any other name." He returned her smile, but his eyes were darkly serious.

For the first time Shelby realized how comfortable she had grown in his company. And it wasn't just the soft night breeze or the wine warming her veins. It had been so long since she had met someone, beyond her immediate circle of colleagues, who intuitively understood the spell of the sea.

It had been so long since a man had looked at her with desire in his eyes.

So long since she had looked at a man that way. Not since the early days with Steve. And the truth was she hadn't even looked at him that way.

Tilting her head back, Shelby focused on the moon-gilded umbrella of leaves rustling overhead. Fragments of an evocative, sweet melody floated past.

"'Tennessee Waltz,'" Jake murmured.

The stars and music and wine were all conspiring to trigger a familiar stirring somewhere deep inside her. This was the right time, the right place, the right mood.

But every ounce of her rational self warned her that Jake Lawson was the wrong man.

Yet as he rose suddenly to his feet, grasping her hand and pulling her into his arms in one swift, certain movement, she realized that her body had its own ideas about Mr. Lawson.

"What are you doing?" she asked breathlessly as her heart surged beneath her sheer blouse.

"Playing a hunch."

Before she could answer, strong arms drew her close, and Jake began swaying gently to the rhythm of the old song.

For a moment she tensed, forcing her body to stiffly ignore Jake's insistent coaxing. But the feel of him—his hand splayed against her back, the rough caress of his jean-covered knee on her thigh—was intoxicating. Gradually she relaxed, moving instinctively as he guided her over the starlit lawn.

How could she have forgotten the magic pleasure of being held like this? There was something . . . protective . . . in his embrace, something that made her feel sheltered and safe. Not that she needed protecting, she reminded herself—it was just a sort of wonderful fringe benefit.

She glanced up to meet Jake's eyes and saw silver moons reflected in their black depths. A faraway smile formed on his wide, sculpted mouth. Slowly she lowered her cheek to rest on his broad chest and inhaled the fresh clean scent of his cotton work shirt, mingling with his after-shave in a seductive blend. Without thinking, she let her fingers play with the thick black curls grazing the back of his collar.

"Not a bad hunch, hmm?" Jake whispered, pulling her closer and slowing his steps.

Everywhere they touched, she melted; and they touched, it seemed, everywhere. Fingers laced, thighs skimmed, hips brushed with tantalizing slowness. When the song ended, it didn't seem to matter. They continued swaying, almost imperceptibly, bodies melded seamlessly. Jake's hard torso pressed against her, teasing her breasts into crested arousal with sweet, calculated precision.

"Shelby," Jake breathed, pulling away slightly to trace the curve of her bottom lip with his index finger. She stood perfectly still, transfixed by his gentleness as he brushed an errant wisp of hair back from her forehead.

She had expected—what? Power, urgency, an impatient, demanding kiss. Something predictable, something she could at least turn aside.

Instead, he was torturing her with a rhythm so hypnotically slow she was drawn in, drowning in sweet, warm eddies of sensation. He brushed her closed eyelids with his lips, cradling her head in his hands, then moved to draw a featherlike path down the curve of her throat before at last venturing toward her mouth.

Even then he took his time, testing her with his patient exploration. With exquisite tenderness he traced her parted lips with his tongue until she moaned with the need to taste him, opening to his quest. Only then, when she'd acknowledged her need, did he kiss her as she'd thought he would: boldly claiming, urgently searching and savoring.

He tasted of adventure and desire and unspoken challenge.

It was delicious, how he tasted.

She freed herself from his touch, breathless and lightheaded.

He tasted dangerous.

She was out of her depth, and sinking fast. Across the lawn the yellow lights of her apartment beckoned reassuringly, a life raft in this sea of frightening uncertainty.

*You can get burned playing hunches, Mr. Lawson.*

"I . . ." she began, wondering what white lie was about to escape her lips. "I really should be getting back to work."

"Work?" He loosened his grip on her shoulders, confusion and frustration darkening his features.

"Song recordings . . . some new data . . ." Lord, she was a terrible liar.

Jake exhaled audibly, jaw muscles working as he considered a response. "If you want to run away, Ms Haynes," he chided, "you don't need to invent excuses."

"I'm not running away," Shelby snapped. "I just need . . ." What *did* she need? "I need more time. Rationally I know it would be a mistake."

"It?"

"You. Me. Us." Her head whirled as she groped for an explanation. "Listen." She touched his arm softly. "For the time being, let's not mix business with pleasure."

"And how long is 'the time being'?"

Shelby drew away, as if putting physical distance between them would be answer enough. She looked around for Cipher, making a show of being distracted.

"Shelby, just how long do we go on not mixing business with pleasure?" Jake demanded.

"For as long as the business lasts," she answered finally.

"But when my business is done . . ." He left the thought unfinished.

"Yes." Shelby nodded. "When your business is done, you'll be leaving." She smiled sadly. "Exactly my point, Captain Lawson." She turned to go. "I'll see you tomorrow."

# 5

JAKE LAWSON STROLLED down Commercial Street at a leisurely pace. He'd been searching halfheartedly for a place to have dinner, but the restaurants were universally jammed and he didn't relish the idea of waiting at a bar by himself, waiting to dine alone. Instead, he'd picked up some fresh swordfish and a few groceries. If he had to eat alone, at least he could do it in the privacy of his own apartment.

It was early evening, but the June sun was still well above the horizon, and the narrow one-way street was jammed with people. Jake realized that he'd come to feel very much at home here in this little village far out to sea.

Cape Cod was shaped like an arm flexing its biceps, and Provincetown was nestled in its half-closed hand, thrust out into the hostile ocean but sheltered from the worst of the elements. On a clear night you could see the faint lights of Boston far off across Cape Cod Bay. It was a compact village, the streets never quite two lanes wide, the buildings never very large or imposing. Everything was on a small scale and utterly lacking in slickness or ostentation. It was a weather-beaten home to flamboyant artists and grizzled fishermen alike, a place overrun by tourists in the summer and retaken by its own quirky residents during the quiet of winter. Yes, he genuinely liked this town, and it wasn't just the influence of his favorite resident.

Several days had passed since he'd danced with Shelby under the stars—several days of cool distance as she stuck to her vow not to mix business and pleasure. Once since then he had asked her to join him for dinner, but she had refused, politely but firmly.

So he had been reduced to watching her as she leaned out over the prow each day, almost like the carved figureheads of women that adorned the old sailing ships. Yet Shelby was no carved image, but a very real woman who had become the focus of more and more of his attention. Heading off to the *Questor* each morning in the early dawn, it was no longer visions of gold that inspired him, but visions of her...Shelby pulling off her earphones and shaking out her golden hair while she stretched like a cat in the sunlight; the look of sudden concentration on her face when she heard through the hydrophones the melancholy song of some far-off whale; the way she'd clapped her hands with delight as a huge humpback breached, leaping high into the air and falling back in slow motion with a tremendous splash.

Jake looked up with a start and realized he'd been day-dreaming. He was farther along than he'd realized. Just up the hill Shelby's Dodge sat parked in front of the yellow Victorian they shared—one of the few things they had in common these days, he reminded himself with a resigned sigh.

As Jake turned into the driveway, Cipher gave a joyful yelp to herald his arrival.

"Hello, boy," Jake said, reaching over the backyard fence to stroke Cipher's ear. "Where's your mistress?"

As if in answer, the door to the upstairs apartment flew open, and Shelby shot down the stairs, two at a time. A stocky, ruddy man followed on her heels. Jake recognized him as Shelby's assistant.

"How far out?" Shelby demanded, rushing toward the back gate.

"Fifty miles, give or take. North, northeast."

"Damn!" Shelby glanced in Jake's direction, but it took several moments before she seemed to register his presence. "Oh," she faltered, "Jake . . ."

"What's going on?"

"Emergency," she said tersely. "Sam just got a call from a tuna boat. They report at least one, maybe two, whales caught in their nets."

Without waiting for a response, she sped down the driveway toward her car with Sam close behind. Jake dropped his grocery bag and broke into a run to catch up with them.

"What about a chopper?" she asked Sam breathlessly when they'd reached the Dodge.

"Dr. Tuan called the Coast Guard. They've agreed to fly us out. Tuan's there sitting on them to make sure they don't change their minds."

Shelby looked at her watch. "Five minutes to get airborne, twenty minutes' flying time." She glanced up at the sky. "We won't have more than fifteen minutes of light. Who else have you got?"

"Just you, me and Tuan. Jack's sick, and I couldn't get hold of Teresa or Kyle."

"We'll just have to make do," Shelby pronounced grimly.

"The weather's clear, at least, but they're reporting three-foot swells and—"

"Oh, no!" Shelby froze. "My gear! My suit and tanks are all out on the *Questor*!"

"Don't look at me." Sam held up his hands. "My extra wet suit wouldn't keep you dry at all. Besides, I only have one regulator."

"If you've got a helicopter, have it swing past the *Questor*. We can winch our gear up on a line."

Shelby turned, startled, as though she had forgotten Jake was there. She hesitated for a moment, then shook her head.

"No choice. We'll have to. But we'll pick up *my* gear, not yours. I've done this before, and it's my job."

"Mind if I come along for the ride, at least?" Jake asked, climbing into the back seat of the car before Shelby could reply.

Shelby settled into the front seat with Sam and revved the engine. "Actually," she said over her shoulder, "I *do* mind, but there's no time to argue now."

THE WHITE Coast Guard helicopter was already beginning to warm up as they ran toward its open door.

Shelby and Sam piled in, with Jake right behind them, and a second later they felt the lurch of takeoff. Inside the close dark belly of the machine, the noise of the turbine engines and the thwack of the rotors was deafening.

A fourth person crouching in the corner leaned forward to extend his hand to Jake. Jake could barely make out the handsome Vietnamese features and the outline of an unlit pipe hanging from the corner of his mouth.

"I'm Dr. Tuan."

Jake shook his hand. "Jake Lawson," he shouted.

The noise was so great that further conversation was impossible, but with hand signs Jake told Shelby he was going forward to the cockpit to radio Greg and Janine aboard the *Questor.*

Moments later the helicopter was hovering over Jake's boat. One of the Coast Guardsmen slid open the door of the chopper and swiveled out a cable winch. Slowly the weighted hook began to descend.

Leaning out, Shelby could see Greg and Janine standing on the deck gazing up at her. Around the boat the wash from the rotors rippled the sea for fifty feet and blew over a plastic cup that had been resting on the fantail. Despite the pilot's efforts to keep their position in the gusting breeze, the hook was soon swinging in a wide arc on the end of thirty feet of played-out cable.

Below them Greg made a couple of fruitless grabs before finally snagging the hook. Together he and Janine tied a pair of oversize canvas duffel bags to the hook. Without waiting for the gear to be fully winched in, the pilot tilted his craft northward.

Shelby was grateful that he understood the need for speed. Whales, as air-breathing mammals, could be drowned when entangling nets held them underwater and kept them from getting their blowholes into the air. If these whales were so badly tangled that they'd been unable to reach the surface at all, then, she realized grimly, they were already dead. Even if they had been able to breathe a little, the constriction and the weight of the nets would soon exhaust them, pulling them under—particularly if they, as so many, were already weakened by the mystery disease. It wouldn't be the first time she'd seen it happen.

As Tuan and Sam pulled on their own wet suits, Shelby began sorting her gear out of one of the duffel bags. She looked up in surprise to see Jake slipping out of his shirt.

"No." She shook her head vigorously.

"Can't hear you," he mouthed, smiling tightly.

"This isn't your problem," she shouted. "You'll just be in the way."

"Good," he shouted back. "Now I can be in *your* way for a change."

But Shelby didn't return his smile. She leaned forward and put her mouth next to his ear to be sure he could hear her. "Don't be foolish. This can be dangerous as hell, and you do not need to impress me this way."

She heard his own voice, now startlingly near. "Always the cynic, aren't you? Besides, you're shorthanded."

When she pulled back, he gave her a wink and mouthed a single word, "Adventure."

Shelby shook her head as if to say, "You don't know what you're getting yourself into," but she couldn't stop the half smile from forming on her lips. It was really awfully hard, she reflected, not to like this man. She inclined her head in tacit acceptance and mouthed, "Be my guest."

Although Jake seemed blithely unconcerned, Shelby and her co-workers were growing increasingly edgy as they helped each other into their tanks. While they made last-minute adjustments to the equipment, Sam nudged Shelby and inclined his head toward Jake, who was whistling happily in the corner. Shelby grinned nervously and gave Sam a conspiratorial look that said wait and see.

Finally the forward thrust of the turbines halted, and the chopper came to a level stop, then began descending slowly toward the water. Sam opened the door onto a startling scene.

The sun was sinking fast, and the surface of the sea sparkled a brilliant gold over the lightless depths below. A hundred yards away a battered wooden fishing boat rose and fell on the swells, while almost directly below the chopper a huge humpback lay unnaturally on its side, one surfboard-size fluke protruding into the air. Peering more closely, Shelby could make out the tangled web of a net.

"She's still alive," Shelby shouted.

"I don't see a second whale," Tuan shouted back.

"Could be trapped underneath," Sam commented and then, catching Shelby's eye, drew her gaze to Jake.

As he poked his head gingerly out of the door to stare at the trapped beast, Jake was looking decidedly pale. Shelby reached around Sam to tap Jake on the shoulder. With hand gestures she made clear to him that he should hold tightly to his face mask when he jumped.

Shelby jumped feet first. It was a fifteen-foot drop to the water from the hovering helicopter—just long enough for her life to flash before her eyes. She hit the water with the impact of a depth charge, fighting to keep her mask in place and struggling to get her mouthpiece firmly between her clenched teeth. Dark water boiled around her, but she quickly got her bearings and regained the surface.

Overhead the helicopter had moved off, climbing to a safer altitude but ready to offer assistance should an emergency arise. Swept up to the crest of a swell, Shelby made a quick head count: Jake nearest, Tuan and Sam swimming around to the far side of the whale.

"Jake!" she shouted, and when he spotted her, she motioned him down. Shelby somersaulted forward and dived down about ten feet, below the surge of the waves. The light was fading fast, but she could clearly see the enormous wall of grayish flesh only a dozen feet away with its deadly swaddling of braided rope.

Jake floated beside her and gave her an okay signal. Pulling her flashlight from her belt, Shelby played the narrow beam around. A dozen feet below the numpback cow she could make out the second whale. It was not moving.

Shelby kicked forward, pulling her knife from the sheath on her right calf, and without hesitation began cutting the thick strands of rope. After watching her lead, Jake descended a couple of feet lower and began working at the net.

The going was tough, and Shelby soon felt herself tiring. There were dozens of strands to be cut, and all the while she was working against the constriction of her wet suit and the resistance of the water.

Suddenly the whale gave a kick, struggling exhaustedly to free itself. The net snapped from Shelby's grip, and she had to shove back from the tortured beast to avoid being badly bruised. After a few seconds the whale seemed to slump and become still again. Shelby returned to its side.

"Where was I?" she asked herself. The scene seemed so confused: there was Jake below her, and the net now drawn taut against the whale. What had she been doing? She shook her head in confusion.

Cutting the net. That was it.

She looked uncomprehendingly at the knife in her hand. It seemed to belong to someone else, and for the life of her she couldn't imagine what it was for.

Somewhere far, far away an alarm was ringing in her mind—a warning she understood but no longer cared about.

The knife slipped from her grip and drifted downward.

Or was it upward? She was no longer sure. Her body seemed to have become separated from her somehow, its muscles useless, beyond control. Slowly she drifted onto her back and began sinking into a black, black well that closed off all light.

JAKE COULD NOT quite believe what he was doing.

What in the name of all that was holy was he doing fifty miles out to sea, sawing through rope to free some behemoth that might just decide at any moment to wriggle its fin, or whatever it was called, and knock his head off?

This was insane! And he was a man with a pretty liberal view of what constituted reasonable behavior.

At least with treasure hunting there was the excuse that one might make a big profit, but this? And yet, he marveled, here he was, frantically sawing away in a race to save the life of this animal the size of a Greyhound bus.

He remembered the reports he'd received from his lawyers on Safeseas's opposition to his salvage permits. They'd had him picturing a group of ecology nuts wearing love beads and living in fern-filled communes.

Well, he was going to have to change law firms.

Whatever you could say about the redoubtable Ms Haynes, she put everything on the line for what she believed in.

Jake glanced up at her, but she was no longer above him. A spike of fear made his breathing stop. He swung to the left and to the right.

She was gone.

Then he noticed a column of bubbles, a wavering line leading like a trail of bread crumbs toward the bottom. There in the gloom he caught the faint glimmer of a chrome regulator.

Jake swooped into a dive, churning the water with all his might as he chased her. She wasn't sinking fast, but still the distance between them closed with infuriating slowness.

He realized that in a moment she would disappear from sight—and she had the only flashlight. Something brushed his hand but slipped away before he could grab it. He was swimming straight down now, thirty feet, forty. He could feel the pressure building and realized that he could no longer see anything.

But she had to be near!

Jake reached into the ink beneath him and felt the thin edge of a flipper. He held it in the most fragile of grips, knowing that if his fingers slipped, or her foot came out, she would be gone.

Desperately he reached forward with his left hand and found her ankle.

His sigh of relief exploded in a cloud of bubbles. She was moving—but weakly, as if in a dream.

Slowly he drew her to him and found her flashlight. He shone the beam into her face mask and saw that her eyes were closed. Working quickly, he tore the mouthpiece from her lips and replaced it with his own. For a moment she didn't respond, and he feared that he was too late. Then he saw the intake of air and knew that she would live.

Holding his own breath, he slipped her unwieldy tanks and weight belt free. As they sank into the invisible depths, he slowly began propelling Shelby toward the surface. Jake knew the compressed air in his own lungs would expand as he rose. He could make it without buddy-breathing, allowing Shelby to retain the mouthpiece and avoid the possibility of inhaling saltwater.

They broke the surface, and Jake, supporting Shelby above the chop, waved to the helicopter overhead. Swooping down, it lowered a body sling, and with the last of his strength Jake fixed the rubber loops under her arms. He watched as she was hauled, swinging gently, to the hovering craft.

A moment later the cable dropped again. Jake breathed an exhausted sigh of relief as he was lifted effortlessly from the deadly sea. Hanging there in space, he could see the great whale thrashing the water and slipping free of the now-severed bonds.

JAKE CLIMBED ABOARD into the relative warmth of the helicopter to find Shelby lying on a blanket, her head propped against a duffel bag. Slowly she nodded her head in answer to a question from the chopper copilot sitting beside her.

"How is she?" Jake demanded, casting aside his flippers and mask and kneeling next to Shelby.

She reached for his shoulder, pulling him so close that he could feel her warm breath against his ear. "She's fine," Shelby assured him weakly, trying to make herself heard over the engine's steady churn.

"A little shocky, maybe," the copilot answered, meeting Jake's worried gaze, "but she seems to be responsive."

Jake arched his brows, grinning knowingly for Shelby's benefit, and she managed a wan grimace in reply.

"I'll get the others now," the copilot shouted to Jake, "if you'll take over here."

Jake nodded seriously. Rummaging through a storage trunk, he unearthed a thick wool blanket. Gently he tucked it around Shelby's rubber-clad body. Reaching beneath the blanket, he found her wrist and withdrew it to check her pulse, staring intently at his watch while he ignored her weak protests.

Satisfied, he leaned close enough for her to hear him. Against her pale skin, her gray eyes glowed with an unnatural sheen, nearly engulfed by her dilated pupils. He swallowed past the unfamiliar knot of fear in his throat.

"Look at me," he commanded, stroking the clammy smoothness of her cheek.

She obeyed, turning her unfocused gaze toward him.

"No pain?"

She shook her head.

Behind them Tuan clambered aboard and made his way to them.

"What happened?" he shouted the question in Jake's ear.

Jake shook his head uncertainly. "Maybe loss of oxygen. No pain."

"Good," Tuan said. "At least it isn't the bends. Is she coherent?" The last word was lost in the howl of the blades as the door opened again to bring Sam on board, but Jake understood his meaning.

"Hey," he shouted hoarsely down at her, "what's the capital of Massachusetts?"

Shelby mumbled something and Jake leaned closer, putting his ear to her lips.

"Provincetown," she answered, smiling weakly.

Jake exhaled a long low sigh of relief. Gently he brushed back a damp strand of hair from her forehead.

"Did we do it?" Shelby asked. Jake turned to Tuan.

"Yes, Miss Haynes," Tuan said. "The cow appears healthy. The young male appears very weak, but is free and moving. I believe he will make it."

Once Sam was safely aboard, the chopper headed for land. The three men changed back into their clothes, then Jake rejoined Shelby. Deftly he eased the duffel bag away and settled behind her, cradling Shelby in his own solid warmth.

Gradually her grogginess began to lift, and as it did, the gravity of her mishap hit her full force. Jake had saved her life, the copilot had told her as he'd pulled her on board the helicopter. There it was, plain and simple: without Jake Lawson, she might not be sitting here right now—in his arms.

She twisted to face him, searching for the right thing to say.

"Better?" he asked, loud enough for her to hear over the chopper's thrashing.

"Shipshape," she answered, suddenly very conscious of his hard arms encircling her body. She could still smell the sea on him, fresh and seductive and dangerous.

He scrutinized her face carefully, then nodded, apparently persuaded.

"Jake . . ." Shelby began, pausing to collect her thoughts. How did you thank somebody for saving your life? Here was one situation Emily Post had definitely overlooked.

Cupping her hands over her mouth, she leaned toward Jake's ear. Glistening black curls grazed her fingers. "I want . . ." she began again, faltering. The words forming on her lips sounded so inadequate and superficial against the magnitude of Jake's act.

He rested the callused tip of an index finger against her lips to silence her, shaking his head almost imperceptibly.

Reluctantly Shelby turned around, easing her back against Jake's chest. Even through her wet suit she could feel the slow, steady throb of his heart. Back on land, she could thank him, and sort out the uncomfortable question of how she could have let this mess happen in the first place. For now she was warm and safe, and that was all that mattered.

ONCE THE CHOPPER HAD LANDED, Shelby was faced with an inevitable insistent chorus of male voices demanding she be checked out by a doctor.

"All I want," she implored, struggling to her feet with Jake's help, "is a warm bath and a warm bed." She brushed aside his steadying arm and stepped toward the door. "And maybe a brandy... or two," she added mischievously.

After changing her clothes and enduring a five-minute face-off with Tuan and Sam, Shelby wrangled a sort of compromise: she could forego the medical evaluation, if she'd allow Jake to see her home and be certain she was safely tucked into bed. Tired as she was, she didn't object too strenuously to the idea of a chaperon, and Jake was perfectly happy to oblige.

Neither spoke during the brief trip home. It wasn't until they were safely upstairs and done greeting an ecstatic Cipher that Shelby, sinking gratefully onto the living-room couch, ventured to speak.

"Jake..." she started, but he was already gone, busily searching through kitchen cupboards.

"Just give me a minute," he called.

He wasn't making things easy.

Moments later he returned to present her with a snifter of brandy.

"Thanks." She smiled gratefully. "What I wanted to say was—"

"Just one more thing," Jake interrupted, striding from the room purposefully.

Shelby sighed, sipping the brandy. From the bathroom came the sound of running water: he was starting a bath for her. In some musty corner of her mind, she felt vaguely uncomfortable about all this unsolicited TLC. Not that there was anything suspect about it. Jake seemed genuinely concerned about her, and that was what bothered Shelby. The kindness in his eyes, the gentle way he'd held her on the chopper trip home, and now all this bustling about for her benefit: it touched her, made her feel vulnerable and needy. Not to mention cared for. Comfortable.

"Your bath awaits," Jake announced, joining her at last on the couch. "Anything else I can do? Your wish is my command."

"I wish," Shelby answered with a hint of defensiveness, "that you'd realize I'm perfectly capable of taking care of myself."

"On that score," Jake said tolerantly, "there has never been any doubt."

"Oh, damn." Shelby set aside her brandy and reached impulsively for Jake's hand. "I don't know where that came from. I'm so sorry. You're being so kind, and it's just that I don't know how to thank you for . . . well, for everything today. If you hadn't been there—"

"Then Tuan or Sam would have," Jake concluded matter-of-factly. "Look. I just grabbed you when you drifted past—nothing more or less than you would have done in the same situation. End of story. The only obligation you have right now is to take that bath and climb into bed so I can tell your co-workers I performed my appointed task."

"You have." Shelby smiled. "Admirably." She released his hand in a flush of self-consciousness. "Consider yourself relieved of duty."

"Not so fast." Jake crossed his arms over his chest. "I'm supposed to have you in bed, fast asleep. That was the deal, as I recall it."

Reluctantly Shelby rose to her feet. "You know, if things don't work out with the *Evangeline*, you might consider a career switch."

"To?" Jake arched a brow.

"Dorm mother."

After a long, lazy bath Shelby, relaxed nearly to the point of immobility, donned one of her oversize T-shirts and climbed into the welcoming warmth of her bed. In the living room she could hear the low drone of the television.

"Okay," she called to Jake. "Mission accomplished."

Seconds later he appeared in the doorway. In the soft yellow light his dark figure dominated the room. Casually he slouched against the doorjamb, smiling broadly. "Bedtime story?" he asked roguishly.

"Thanks, no. I'll pass out as soon as my head hits the pillow."

Jake gestured toward the wicker rocker next to her bed. "May I?"

"If you want."

He settled into the rocker, suddenly pensive. "Shelby," he finally asked softly, stroking his jaw, "what do you think went wrong out there?"

The question caught her off guard; she'd been trying very hard not to think about the mishap. "I don't know, Jake." She sighed. "I'm a good, experienced diver. Really I am. I checked the pressure gauge after we brought up the tanks and they were full. Besides, I wasn't out of air—I would have noticed that."

"Did you refill them after your last dive—personally?"

Shelby thought a moment, then nodded slowly. "Yes. I remember it. So I guess I must have screwed up somehow. The only thing I can think of is carbon-monoxide contamination."

"It can't be much else," Jake agreed. "Which means one of three things. Either the compressor filter is bad, or the intake may be too close to the exhaust or—"

"Or it was deliberately tampered with," Shelby finished the thought. "But that would be attempted murder, Jake," she said, dismissing the notion. "No, I'm the one who filled those tanks, and I wasn't familiar with that compressor model. I've got no one to blame but myself."

Jake looked down at the floor for a long moment, as though debating the matter internally. Finally he said, "Well, tomorrow I'll have Thomas go over that compressor—change the filter and make sure it's not taking in its own exhaust. Or to hell with it—I'll get a whole new unit." He stood up, stretching his back, and gazed down at her.

"You know, I think you're one of the few genuinely brave people I've ever met in my life," Jake mused, almost to himself.

She met his eyes and saw he was absolutely serious. "Don't get out much, do you?" she responded in embarrassment, her cheek hot against the cool cotton pillowcase.

"Enough to know when someone deserves my respect." Jake flicked off the light on her nightstand. "I'll take Cipher out, then lock up. And don't worry about your alarm. Tomorrow's a holiday."

"But—"

"I need some work done on the engines, Ms Haynes. You think I'd sacrifice a perfectly good day so you can catch up on your beauty sleep?" He rose, and even in the darkness she could make out his smile. "Not that you need it, mind you."

The touch of his lips against her forehead was so tender and fleeting that in the morning she couldn't be sure she hadn't dreamed it.

# 6

EVEN AFTER TEN LUXURIOUS HOURS of sleep, Shelby awoke the next morning groggy and bone tired. Jake's protest notwithstanding, she felt certain the unscheduled day off for the *Questor* crew was entirely for her benefit. And to be honest, she was grateful for the free time. The rescue effort had taken its toll physically, and she could put the afternoon to good use over at the Safeseas office.

It was nearly two by the time Shelby arrived at work. Colleagues in the cluttered front office greeted her with applause and cheers.

"C'mon, you guys," Shelby groaned, "I'm none the worse for wear. But I do hope you'll all keep what nearly happened to me in mind when you're diving. Remember—there are old divers, and there are careless divers, but—"

"But," Teresa completed the homily, "there are no old, careless divers. Yeah, we know. But no more object lessons from you, all right?"

"Deal," Shelby agreed enthusiastically.

"Why aren't you out looking for buried treasure?" Teresa asked as they slipped into the relative privacy of Shelby's office.

"Jake declared a day off."

"That was nice of him."

"Uh-huh," Shelby said noncommittally.

"Then why aren't you at home, recuperating, instead of in here?"

"Oh, just my usual saintlike dedication to duty," Shelby joked.

"Right." Teresa rolled her eyes. "So what happened? Did you try to fill your tanks from your car's tail pipe again?"

"Very funny."

"No, not very funny," Teresa said, suddenly serious. "You get yourself killed out there, and I will personally kill you. You're the best friend I have."

"Thanks. I think."

"Besides . . ." Teresa began again, but Shelby held up a hand. "Please, no more lectures."

"No more lectures," her friend agreed. "Something more important. Filene's is having a big sale. I called yesterday morning to invite you to drive down with me to the mall tomorrow, but as you know, your answering machine and I are not on speaking terms."

Shelby laughed. "Teresa, isn't it time you joined the twentieth century?"

"Someone has to dig in and fight the march of progress. So, tomorrow? I'll drive."

"Okay, maybe. But call and remind me tonight or I'll forget." Teresa turned to go. "And if I'm out, leave a message on the machine for me," Shelby shouted as her friend closed the door. Moments later she heard Teresa's defiant voice.

"Never!"

SHELBY SCRIBBLED ABSENTLY on the notepad before her. She'd spent most of the afternoon going over reports on whale fatalities—reports she'd gone over a dozen times before, always looking for the clue that would leap out at her and provide all the answers. But by late afternoon the words had begun to blur, and the little room was closing in on her.

Most of her co-workers had left, but she felt duty-bound to stay, even though she was getting next to nothing accomplished, sitting there doodling stick figures.

*Stop wasting time and get to work*, she chided herself. *Tomorrow you'll have to be back out there on the* Questor.

She tried hard to make the prospect seem unpleasant, but into her mind came the scent of the open sea, the gentle rise and fall of the swells, the awareness of Jake gazing down from his bridge....

Oh, this was hopeless. She closed the folder on her desk and returned it to her drawer. She would go home, heat up a TV dinner and come back later when she'd got her second wind.

The front door to the office opened, and she heard footsteps in the hallway outside.

"Sam?" she shouted.

Her door opened and Jake strode in. "No. Just me. Disappointed?" He was wearing what she'd now come to think of as his uniform: tight-fitting denims and a blue chambray shirt. Somehow, on Jake, the combined effect was just short of devastating.

He settled in a chair, slouching comfortably.

She wanted to tell him that no, she was not at all disappointed. "Welcome to my humble domain," she said.

"Nice." He smiled wryly, glancing around the room. "So this is the nerve center of the operation."

"Yep." Shelby laughed. "It's dingy, overcrowded and messy, but we pretend to love it, anyway."

"How are you doing?" Jake asked, becoming serious.

"I'm hungry, I feel like the walls are closing in on me and I have a headache."

"I told you you should have seen a doctor," Jake reproached her.

"No, no. It's not that. I feel fine, really," Shelby said, touched by his concern. "It's just been a tough day."

"Well, then. One, if you're hungry, you should eat. Two, if the walls are closing in, you should get fresh air. And," he lowered his voice suggestively, "three, if you have a headache, you should let me rub your neck."

"All three at once?"

"Strangely enough, yes. I was just dropping by to see how you feel about picnics. But be careful how you answer." He raised a warning finger. "It's practically subversive not to like picnics."

"Well, I don't know," Shelby hesitated. "One sounds good. Two sounds okay, but I'm not sure about three."

"You're not afraid, are you?" he prodded.

"Should I be?" she fired back.

"Not of me," he said softly. "Come on, I promise I'll be a good boy." His solemn expression earned a grudging laugh. He reached across the desk for her hand, and at his warm touch her remaining hesitation evaporated.

"Okay, okay. I guess we can stop off at the market on the way."

Jake shook his head. "All taken care of. It's in the car."

Shelby gave him a dubious look. "When did you plan all this?"

"I ordered it this morning."

"Sure of yourself, aren't you?"

"If I'm not, who will be?"

THE SUN WAS ALREADY LOW on the horizon by the time they parked the car at the visitors' center and began the slow trek across the sand, carrying a huge picnic basket between them.

"My sources tell me we should hoof westward till we collapse," Jake explained.

"That might not be far, carrying this basket. We could feed a small army."

After a few clumsy steps both removed their shoes, half-filled with sand. The sloping, sun-baked dunes were still warm against their bare soles, and the breeze that whispered past them was ocean seasoned. The sound of the gulls sailing above mingled with the softly crashing surf.

"Tired?" Jake asked as they slogged on across the too-yielding sand.

"Didn't anyone ever tell you women have more endurance than men?"

"I'm planning an independent scientific study on just that question. Want to volunteer?"

"Thanks. I've had my fill of scientists." She hoped he would let the remark pass.

He did.

They descended into a narrow pocket formed by two adjoining dunes. "This is it, I think," Jake said. "The perfect spot. Protected on three sides, with a great view of the sunset. And quite secluded." He set down the picnic basket and reached for her hand. "How about a walk along the shore?"

"Are you forgetting the ten-mile hike we just took?" she objected. There was a seriousness, an intensity to him that made her suddenly wary, but his voice remained reassuringly nonchalant.

"You were saying about endurance?" he challenged, dropping her hand and racing to the water's edge.

She followed suit, nearly colliding with him as the ocean foamed around her toes. Jake caught her, panting, and she let herself be suspended in his strong embrace for just a minute before breaking free. They began a slow stroll along the wet, cool sand, skirting the edge of the breaking surf. From time to time Shelby stooped to pick up a shell and show it to Jake.

The huge ochre sun retreated behind towering mounds of cumulus clouds balancing on the horizon like piles of overstuffed pillows. Color seeped into them, separating into a spectrum from palest lilac to bloodred.

"A perfect Cape Cod sunset," Jake pronounced.

"Did you plan this, too?"

"I'm afraid I can't take any credit. Think we should turn back?"

"Sure. I've worked up quite an appetite."

They retraced their steps, most of which had been erased by the patient sea.

"I suppose you grow pretty blasé about all this—" he waved an arm that included the dunes, the waves and the setting sun "—when you live here all the time."

"Not much like Texas, I guess." Shelby smiled.

Jake nodded. "Not much."

"Not much like Baltimore, either."

"Baltimore? Really?" Jake laughed. "I thought you just kind of sprang out of the ocean one day. A mermaid who'd given up her tail."

"Hmm. I kind of like that idea, but no. I grew up in Baltimore, but every summer my family spent a week on the Cape. I learned to swim before I could walk." She smiled wistfully, losing herself to the memory. "My brothers taught me to snorkel when I was four. A real prodigy."

"Brothers? Plural?"

"Three of them, all older." She watched a grin form on Jake's lips. "Yes, I *was* a bit of a tomboy. Not exactly NFL material, but I held my own playing touch football Sunday afternoons."

"I'm impressed."

"And I think they were good for me. Made me . . . more sure of myself, more independent than some of my friends. Of course," she added with a self-deprecating laugh, "my mom despaired for me. She was certain I'd never settle down."

"It appears she may have had a point."

Shelby caught a note of admiration in his tone and felt strangely gratified. How, she wondered, had she wandered so casually into this rocky emotional terrain? Still, her inability to "settle down" seemed to be something Jake could understand.

"I am settled, in a way," she continued. "But grants come and go, and Safeseas isn't exactly rolling in money. So even if I'm not in Provincetown forever, I'll be happy as long as I can keep my research on track."

"The important thing is that you love your work."

Shelby smiled. "I wish you would explain that to my mother. I mean, don't get me wrong, my family's very supportive, but I think my mom's a little uncomfortable when she tries to explain to the bridge club why her daughter hangs around whales for a living."

Jake nodded sympathetically. "You think that's bad. Try making 'treasure hunter' sound respectable!"

"Respectable? No. Glamorous, maybe. Or exotic."

"I'll go along with exotic," Jake agreed. "So mind if I ask you a question?"

She laughed. "Probably."

"What have you, of all people, got against scientists?" His tone was light but carried the hint of more-than-passing interest.

Shelby had discussed her relationship with Steve so rarely that she scarcely knew where to start. "Not scientists plural." She hesitated. Did he really want to hear the story of her life? And did she really want to tell it? But looking into his eyes, she saw only concerned interest—an expression that seemed to say, "You can talk to me. I've made my own mistakes, suffered my own emotional defeats." Jake remained silent, waiting for her to decide whether to go on.

"Not scientists plural," she repeated. "A scientist, singular. My ex-husband." She paused. It was hard to explain, hard to put feelings into words. Yet somehow, strangely, here, now, the whole tawdry, painful tale didn't seem to matter quite as much. Maybe it *was* time to put it behind her.

"We worked together in Florida," she began.

"And?" Jake prompted gently. They turned inward toward the twin dunes where their picnic basket lay nestled.

"And then . . . we fell in love. Or at least I thought we did . . . and got married."

"Let me guess." Jake deliberately injected a teasing note. "He was only interested in your body?"

"No." Shelby laughed wryly. "Not Steve. Oh, that was part of it, of course, but what Steve really wanted was an assistant. Someone to be a mother to his crayfish, someone to type his—"

"Excuse me?" Jake interrupted, stopping dead in his tracks. "Did you say crayfish?"

"Orconectes Limosus, to be precise. The stuff of great love affairs. I spent two years watching a tankful of crayfish and taking notes. How they swam, how they ate, how they fought, how they mated. Believe me, if you ever need to know anything about crayfish, I'm the woman to see." She shook her head at the memory. "Lord, was I sick of those things."

"I can imagine."

"I used to see them in my sleep."

"And Steve?" Jake prompted her again.

"Steve?" she repeated dully. "He wrote a paper on them, which got him a nice fat grant. All in his name, as it turned out. No mention of the poor dumb chump who did all the work."

Together they spread their blanket over the rapidly cooling sand. Jake opened a bottle of wine and poured it into two crystal glasses, then helped Shelby lay out a tempting array of foods.

"When I decided to research whale songs," Shelby continued a while later, sampling a large ripe strawberry, "things *really* went downhill. As long as I labored in Steve's shadow, we coasted along. But when I exchanged my lab coat for a wet suit, it was all over. It was too dangerous, he said, but what he meant was too independent."

Jake nodded, as though he now understood something that had previously eluded him.

"So, anyway, Steve's in Boston now, working for the state. He's a consultant with the Environmental Protection Department." She shook her head. "Sounds like my kind of guy, huh? I guess what hurt was that I could have been so wrong about him. We were so alike, superficially at least. Same interests, same background, same occupation, same tastes."

Jake placed a slice of pâté on a cracker and handed it to her. "Is that important, being so much alike?"

"I thought it was at the time." She laughed ruefully. "You know, it's hard to believe, but in three years' time we never fought. Even our breakup was polite. In the best traditions of scientific reason and emotional discipline."

"Sounds dull." Jake handed her a trimmed wedge of cheese. "Arguing can be good for the soul. Not to mention the fun of making up."

"Are you speaking from firsthand experience?"

Jake sipped from his wineglass. "Just a hunch," he answered, a smile tugging at one corner of his mouth until the dimple in his cheek appeared.

It made, Shelby mused, an utterly charming addition to his features.

"So I can safely assume you've never taken the matrimonial plunge?" she ventured.

"Came close." He chewed on a carrot stick, oddly pensive. "I, uh, abandoned ship at the last moment."

"Not . . . at the altar?" Shelby gasped.

"Oh, no, no." Jake laughed sheepishly. "Nothing like that. I was engaged to a very nice, sensible young lady from Fort Worth who wanted 2.2 kids, a white picket fence and a husband with a nice, sensible job."

"That doesn't sound like you."

"No—" he shrugged "—but it *was* me for a while. I was her boy next door—business degree from the University of Texas, served a hitch in the army like every other man in the Lawson clan, entered my father's real-estate business. The perfect match, really." He paused to prepare plates of crisp fried chicken and potato salad and handed one to Shelby.

"What went wrong?" she pressed.

"Well, things seemed to go bad about the time I sold everything I owned and bought a boat—in Barbados. That wasn't exactly in the script as far as Carol was concerned. I asked her to go with me—marry me on the high seas or some such thing. Naturally she thought I'd been drinking." His mouth twisted into a self-mocking smile. "Truth is, I think I had been."

"Why?" Shelby asked, taking a bite from a drumstick.

"Why was I drinking?"

"No, why did you sell everything you owned and buy a boat?"

Jake stroked his mustache thoughtfully. "My dad had this old map, supposedly handed down from a cavalry scout, who'd gotten it off a dying chief of the Yaqui, who'd had it passed down from the days of the Aztecs. . . . Well, you get the idea. Anyway, this map claimed to show where there was a great cache of gold that the Aztecs had hidden from the conquistadores—a fake, of course." He frowned, and minutes plodded by before he continued. "I think my father knew all along it was bogus, but he kept it in his wall safe, and as long as I can remember, he used to talk about how someday. . .

"To make a long story short, he never did get around to trying out that map. There was always the family, the office. One thing or another. One day I was sitting there at my desk, talking about mortgage rates or some such baloney, and I saw my dad in his office with his head down on his desk, like he was asleep. Only he wasn't asleep." He sighed, staring out into the distance. "I still have the map. I'm about ninety percent sure it's fake." He gave her a sidelong glance. "But the truth is, I don't really want to find out."

Shelby reached for his hand and squeezed it gently.

"I could see my own future laid out right there before me. Interest rates, and closing costs, and termite inspections till someday a stroke got me, and my son inherited my own wasted dreams."

The look in his eyes had grown defiant. "So, Shelby Haynes, I said, 'the hell with this,' and I sold the business. Last I heard, Carol was happily married and expecting her fourth child. And the rest, as they say, is history."

Jake leaned back against the blanket and watched the clouds, now the deep purple of a ripe plum, shift and swirl in a lazy tempo. "You know, there must be a dessert in that basket somewhere."

"Are you nuts? I'm stuffed! I may never move again as it is." She returned the remaining food to the basket and replenished their glasses. Jake lay quietly, one arm behind his head, lost in private thoughts.

She had begun to understand what made the enigmatic Captain Lawson tick. Beneath the tough facade, he was remarkably like her at heart. A bit of a renegade, with a need to carve out a special niche all his own. A man afraid to get lost in other people's expectations.

She pushed the basket away and lay down next to him on the blanket.

Beyond them the ocean surged, steady and strong as a heartbeat. Jake lay inches from her, deep in contemplation, his features indistinct in the dwindling light. She heard his breathing, woven through the ocean's soft churning like counterpoint, rhythmic and hypnotic.

The wine had relaxed the muscles of her back and neck, stiff from an afternoon of poring over paperwork. Closing her eyes, she listened to the wind in the sea grass and the faraway calls of the gulls. Time slipped away as she forgot all but the breeze-borne sounds and the feel of the sand beneath their blanket, molded to the contours of her body.

Gradually she became aware of a change in Jake's breathing. She heard a stirring beside her, a tug at the blanket as he shifted position. Even with her eyes closed Shelby knew he was watching her. She could imagine his gaze as a touch, lighting here . . . there.

The sound of the sea faded and became the sound of her own heart, nearer and more insistent. She heard Jake draw a breath to speak.

"Shelby. . ." he began. His voice came from deep within his chest.

Still, she kept her eyes closed to his nearness. To see was to think, and to reason and to doubt, and her body did not, at this moment, care much for reason.

He touched her cheek, cool fingertips memorizing its fiery contours. "You know," he whispered huskily, "sometimes being cautious is the biggest mistake we can make. I know that all too well."

His voice was a narcotic, as soft and seductive as a lullaby.

"I'm not Steve, Shelby. I don't want you to make compromises." He combed her hair with trembling fingers. "I don't want to change your life."

She felt the gentle moistness of his lips caress her closed lids.

"The greater the risk, Shelby—" warm breath teased her lips, perilously close "—the greater the rewards."

She felt his lips on hers, the warm trespass of his tongue, the slight shiver of his self-restraint. Shelby didn't allow herself to answer his urgency, but deep within her she felt a sudden, flaring heat, like a fuse igniting.

"See what I mean?" Jake asked thickly.

He didn't wait for an answer but lowered his head to kiss the throbbing pulse at the base of her neck, testing her arousal. Satisfied, he moved lower, and Shelby knit her fingers into the soft waves of his hair, struggling for breath. She felt the heat of his mouth through the thin fabric of her blouse as he circled the swell of her breasts, spurning their peaked offering. She arched herself toward him, but he withdrew, and his refusal was wind on a glowing ember.

Shelby felt him move over her, kneeling so that her hips were caught in the vise of his hard thighs. His finger touched her lips, and she kissed its tip before he trailed it down the line of her throat to the pulsing spot that marked her heart. The tug of fabric tightening across her chest told her he'd released the first button of her blouse.

Three more, and he paused, waiting until the ocean's own breath lifted the filmy fabric like a fallen leaf and left her bare.

Gently his hands encircled her breasts, warming and lifting her to him. With one hand he imprisoned a swollen nipple, while his mouth engulfed the other, teasing, swirling, tasting.

The fire in her belly spread and consumed, sucking away precious air, burning away her self-control. She freed the buttons of Jake's shirt, unable to stop the hands that traveled every inch of his powerful shoulders, that raked the sinews of his back, that searched for and found the hard nipples nearly lost in the rough hair of his chest.

Their mouths met, and this time she did not hold back.

When at last he broke free, trembling, Shelby opened her eyes to see him outlined against the canopy of twilight stars above her.

It was so easy to want him. It would be so easy to give in to the insistent demands of her body.

And when he was gone? When he sailed away with his gold and jewels and left her here?

His lips traced a path of kisses along the inside of her wrist.

How could she survive, when he left with the treasure—and her heart, as well?

"Jake," she whispered.

"Yes, love?"

What could she say? How could she explain the cold, raw fear in her heart?

"Jake," she said again. Her eyes glossed with hot tears. "I don't want to need what I can't have."

"Just what is that supposed to mean?"

"It means I don't want to spend my life looking off to the horizon, waiting to see if you'll ever come back."

"Are you so sure I'll leave?" he asked softly.

"I'm sure you'll...have to leave," she managed to say. "I'm sorry, really I am. It's just that you're ... too much. It took me long enough to get over Steve, and he was . . . he wasn't you."

"That's just the point," Jake answered, studying her eyes for something he could not find in her words. "By expecting the past to repeat itself, you're destroying the present. *Our* present."

Gently he pressed against her. The night breeze had grown chill, and Shelby welcomed the warm blanket of his chest in spite of herself. She turned her head away to avoid his searching gaze. Only when she felt Jake brushing them away did she notice the hot tears spilling from her eyes.

"Please, Shelby," Jake began, his breath cool on her hot, wet cheek, "please. I can't give you guarantees."

She swallowed hard. "Maybe someday I won't need them."

Jake pulled away slowly, almost uncertainly. He looked down at her, anger warring with unabated desire, but when he spoke, his tone was resigned. "You know, I almost wish I could tell you that this is it, but I can't. Because I think you're worth the risk, Shelby. Worth risking the pain for." He began buttoning his shirt. "Someday I hope you'll decide I'm worth the risk, too."

They dressed in silence. Jake stuffed the remnants of their picnic into the basket with quick impatient gestures, and they began the long, slow walk across the cooling sand.

Neither of them spoke during the ride back to town. When Jake snapped on his radio and the last few bars of the "Tennessee Waltz" broke the eerie silence, it seemed to Shelby that she had never in her life heard a sadder melody.

JAKE SLAMMED THE DOOR to his apartment with more force than was necessary. Heading to his bedroom, he kicked off his shoes and fell back on the bed.

Above him, as if not to be outdone, he heard the sharp report of Shelby's door as she yanked it shut.

He could map her movements by the sounds penetrating his ceiling. He heard pacing . . . the creak of a chair . . . more pacing. Just a few inconsequential feet above him she roamed like a dare. Even now he could see himself climbing that interior staircase, two—no, three—steps at a time. Jake pounded the bed in frustration, leaping to his feet.

He caught an unnerving glimpse of his image in the bureau mirror. His jaw muscle contracted involuntarily. A pulse churned urgently at his temple. His eyes were black, unfathomable depths: someone else's eyes.

Shelby still paced upstairs. Close enough to hear. He reached a hand up over his head. Almost close enough to touch.

Did she have any idea he was down here listening so intently? Could she even begin to suspect how fully, almost painfully aroused he was?

No, Jake, no.

He remembered their drive home, the two of them engulfed in silence. Their encounter on the beach had sent them both veering off into separate memories, licking separate wounds.

He was being a damned fool, pursuing Shelby this way. She'd been burned once before; she needed time. It was that simple. If and when she was ready, she would let him know.

But the very qualities that had scared off her ex-husband—Shelby's spirit, her independence—were what made her so irresistible to him. They were two people forged from the same metal. He ached to tell her that, but words were not exactly his greatest strength.

Oh, well, a lot of things ached lately. He would just have to give her time, and hope she came around. And if she didn't?

Upstairs he heard a rush of water running through pipes, heard footsteps, now barefoot, and the noise of a glass door rolling open, then back.

She was taking a shower.

The realization conjured up a mental image that made him groan. Once more, despite his rationalizations, he considered bounding up those tempting stairs.

Instead, he headed for his own shower, grimly determined to make it a very cold one.

# 7

"OH, STOP FEELING GUILTY and get in," Teresa said, hands on hips. "You can't work all the time."

"Okay," Shelby agreed meekly, climbing into the little yellow subcompact.

"Shopping is good for the soul," Teresa said, getting behind the wheel. "And a little mindless pleasure will be good for you."

"Yeah—" Shelby smiled obliquely as the engine started to purr "—where have I heard that line before?"

"Where?" Teresa prompted with sudden interest.

"That was a rhetorical question, Terry."

"Oh," she said glumly. "I was afraid of that."

Despite Shelby's initial hesitation, once they were out of town and on Highway 6, she was glad Teresa had pressured her into taking a trip to the mall in Hyannis. As much as she loved P-town, it could get a little confining at times. There were moments when one wanted a little less cute and a little more crass.

The traffic wasn't bad, for a weekend, although when they arrived at the mall forty minutes later, parking was at a premium. The sale at Filene's had attracted a good crowd of locals, summer residents and tourists. After a few minutes' browsing through a rack of pastel dresses, Shelby found herself wandering toward the sportswear section. She held up a cotton rugby shirt for Teresa's opinion, but her friend just rolled her eyes toward heaven.

"Shel, honey, what you don't need are any more sensible, comfortable clothes that can stand exposure to saltwater."

"But it's only $12.95."

"And it will just do wonders for your figure," Teresa drawled. "And it will go just perfectly with your forty-seven pairs of jeans."

"I don't have forty-seven pairs of jeans." Shelby laughed self-consciously.

"How many?"

"Mmm..." Shelby pursed her lips. "Six, I think. No, seven, if you count the ones I painted the bathroom in."

"And how many T-shirts?"

"A couple of dozen, but—"

"A couple of dozen," Teresa repeated, "and if I remember correctly, a grand total of one nice dress, which, incidentally, I've never seen you wear."

Shelby hung her head, feigning embarrassment, even as she returned, undeterred to the rugby shirt. "But it's only $12.95."

"Fine. Be that way." Teresa threw up her hands. "But ask yourself this," she lowered her voice silkily, "do you really want *him* to see you in things like that?"

"Him? Who him? Him who?" Shelby babbled unconvincingly. "To whom are you referring...to?"

Teresa put her nose in the air and began strolling away nonchalantly. "The 'him who' who orders picnic baskets from the gourmet shop. That's the him to whom I'm referring...to."

"How do you know about that?" Shelby asked lamely, following her.

"I have my spies, fortunately, because my best friend—" she gave Shelby an accusing look "—tells me nothing."

"There's nothing to tell. We had a picnic."

"Where?"

Shelby waved a hand vaguely. "On the beach somewhere."

"It was a crowded beach, mademoiselle?" Teresa essayed a French accent and twirled an imaginary mustache. "I caution you, do not attempt to deceive me. Hercule Poirot is no fool."

"Not very crowded, no."

"Deserted, perhaps? *Oui, bien sûr*, it was deserted. Perhaps under a full moon? Or no, better yet, sunset."

"What did you do, follow us?" Shelby scowled.

"All right, Shelby," Teresa dropped the accent. "Spill it."

"We had a picnic. On the beach. At sunset."

"And?"

"And we talked."

"And?"

"He . . . he may have kissed me."

"A little brotherly peck on the forehead or a great big, full-power, steam-coming-out-of-your-ears—"

Shelby couldn't repress a giggle at the image. "Terry," she sighed at last, "there was steam enough to parboil a couple of lobsters."

"Now we're getting somewhere." Teresa rubbed her hands. "Then what?"

"Then we went home."

"And?"

"No 'and.'" Shelby shook her head.

"All right. Now I don't want to pry—"

"Since when?"

"But which of you put the brakes on the 'and'? Never mind. Don't answer. It had to have been you."

"I'm . . . I'm just not ready for that much involvement again." Shelby grew serious. "Lord knows, I wanted to . . . continue the other night, but—"

"But what?"

"But sexual attraction isn't everything."

"*Is* it everything?" Teresa turned the question around. "Or isn't there already something more?"

Shelby began absently fingering a circular rack of silk blouses. "He . . ." she began, then hesitated. "No, it isn't everything. If it was, I could deal with it. But Jake . . . Jake is so . . ." She gestured with her hands as though trying to draw words out of the air. "When Jake's in the room, I feel . . . I feel this kind of sappy smile forming. I have to fight to keep from going into a kind of daze. I mean, it takes real effort for me to be angry at him sometimes."

"Well, we can't have that, can we?"

But Shelby scarcely heard her remark. "I can't stop thinking about him. Wondering if he's thinking about me. Wondering if I'll ever stop thinking about him—" the thought made her wince as if with physical pain "—even when he's gone."

"Ah, so that's it."

"Yes, that's it." Shelby shook her head to drive off the sudden surge of emotion.

"Shelby, Shelby. Don't you know it's better to have loved and lost than never to have loved at all?"

The line had the desired effect of coaxing a smile. "Oh, please," Shelby said, "don't start hitting me with platitudes. Besides, I've already loved and lost."

Teresa grimaced. "Steve just used you to get what he wanted. You don't think Jake . . ." she trailed off.

Shelby was silent for a long moment. "I wonder," she said at last.

"What does your intuition tell you?"

Shelby made a wry grin. "I'm not sure, my friend. But—" she held up a finger "—I have decided one thing."

"Oh?"

"Yes. I've decided to pass on the rugby shirt."

Teresa headed back toward the rack. "Oh, good. 'Cause I wanted it, and it's the only one left in that size."

SHELBY HUDDLED in the launch, reminding herself she had never gotten seasick and was not about to start at this point in her career.

The ride out to the *Questor* did not bode well for the day to come—but then, why should today be any different? At least it was Friday. A mass of clouds hung low on the horizon, and the launch leaped and bucked on the choppy sea, delivering one stomach-wrenching impact after another.

Shelby zipped up her windbreaker and wiped the mist of salt spray from her cheeks. Just ahead she could make out a dark silhouette on the *Questor*'s flying bridge, hands on hips, staring out to sea.

Jake.

It had been a week since their picnic on the beach, and still her heart missed a few beats each time she saw him. On board the boat they had developed a sort of civil shorthand: polite inquiries, choreographing coffee breaks at different times, speaking through intermediaries.

After work they went their separate ways—she, straight home to a frozen dinner and an evening spent drowning herself in work. She was getting nowhere on the whales' illness, every lead turning into a dead end. Yet it kept her preoccupied while she listened for the sound of Jake's car in the driveway.

The first few nights he'd come home late, around midnight, although she'd tried desperately not to check the clock when she heard his car door slam. Last night she hadn't heard him come home at all—at least not by the wee hours of the morning when she'd finally dropped off.

If only she had shut out her doubts, she could have been happy there on the beach with only the moon above to hold her accountable. He had made her feel the urgent need to administer pleasure, the sweet, selfish joy of surrender.

But there had been too much hard tenderness in his eyes, and too much aching need in her own heart. She wanted him far, far too much. And if she gave in to her own desires, even for one night, she would never be able to stop wanting him.

So that when he left—and he *would* leave—the pain would be unbearable.

They pulled alongside the *Questor*, and Greg and Janine, who were already aboard, waved cheerfully. Shelby returned what she hoped would pass for a smile and stole a surreptitious glance at the bridge.

Jake was just turning away, his face preoccupied and tired, but his gaze locked with hers for a second that paralyzed time, before at last, as though by common agreement, the moment was broken.

All week the *Questor* had been running a geometric search pattern, towing its array of equipment over the square mile of ocean where Shelby had stumbled on their one find. On the bridge Janine or Thomas or one of the others would watch the sidescan sonar, trying to pick the image of a hull out of the shadows on the ocean floor. From time to time divers were sent down to check on a reading that inevitably turned out to be nothing more than a sunken fishing boat or a small reef.

The only excitement had come the day before. They had been towing the magnetometer as usual but had ventured a little way out of their normal grid when the cable had suddenly snapped. Before anyone could react, the magnetometer had been lost.

After checking the break in the cable line, Jake had returned to the bridge without a word to calmly order a replacement. Shelby had managed to get a look at the cable, and to her eyes it looked like a suspiciously clean break—rather more like a cut through two-thirds of the thickness while the remaining strands, too weak to bear the strain, had gradually unraveled and snapped. Shelby knew that Jake would have the same suspicions she now had, but he hid his doubts behind a stone face that did not invite speculation.

He knew, she realized, but he did not want to know. Because the minute he admitted that there might be a saboteur aboard the *Questor*, the trust he shared with his crew would be poisoned.

She wondered for the dozenth time if she had been right to withhold her suspicions about the scuba tanks, but on balance she felt she had been. Whoever the saboteur was, he was clever, and forcing the matter into the open would not help catch the one responsible. For now she could only keep her eyes open and hope the hidden enemy made a mistake.

THE DAY WORE ON, and Shelby was beginning to pray for a lunch break when two fan-shaped spouts blew only a hundred yards ahead.

"Stop engines!" she shouted. There was no response, and the steady throb of the diesels continued undiminished.

"I said, stop engines!"

This time the engines died, and the *Questor*'s momentum quickly fell away.

Just fifty yards in front of her Shelby made out the huge outlines of a female humpback and her calf.

"What's the problem?"

She knew the voice instantly and hesitated before turning to answer.

# You may already have won the

# MILLION DOLLAR GRAND PRIZE!

## Harlequin Reader Service®

## Sweepstakes Entry Form

This is your **unique**
Sweepstakes Entry Number:     4A 772751

This could be your lucky day! If you have the winning number, you could be the Grand Prize Winner. To be eligible, *affix Sweepstakes Entry Sticker here!*

If you would like a chance to win the $35,000.00 prize, the $10,000.00 prize, or one of the many $5,000.00, $1,000.00, $500.00, or $5.00 prizes ... plus the Cadillac and the Vacation of a Lifetime, *affix Cash and Bonus Prize Sticker here!*

To receive free books and gifts with no obligation to buy, as explained in the advertisement, *affix the Free Books and Gifts Sticker here!*

142 CIH MDS2

Please enter me in the sweepstakes and tell me if I've won the $1,000,000.00 Grand Prize! Also tell me if I've won any other cash prize, or the car, or the vacation prize. And ship me the free books and gifts I've requested with the sticker above. Entering the sweepstakes costs me nothing and places me under no obligation to buy! (If you do not wish to receive free books and gifts, do not affix the FREE BOOKS and GIFTS sticker.)

| YOUR NAME | | PLEASE PRINT | |
|---|---|---|---|
| ADDRESS | | | APT. # |
| CITY | | STATE | ZIP |

Offer limited to one per household and not valid for current Temptation subscribers.

PRINTED IN U S A

DETACH ALONG DOTTED LINE _ _ P.O. Box 1867, Buffalo, N.Y. 14269-1867.

DETACH ALONG DOTTED LINE

NO POSTAGE
NECESSARY
IF MAILED
IN THE
UNITED STATES

## BUSINESS REPLY MAIL
FIRST CLASS    PERMIT NO. 717    BUFFALO, NY

POSTAGE WILL BE PAID BY ADDRESSEE

**HARLEQUIN READER SERVICE®**
MILLION DOLLAR SWEEPSTAKES
901 Fuhrmann Blvd.
P.O. Box 1867
Buffalo, NY 14240-9952

"There's a mother and calf right up ahead there." She met Jake's gaze for only a moment. His jaw was darkened by a neglected five o'clock shadow. She turned back to point—unnecessarily. The huge pair were hard to miss.

"Oh. Well, how long are they going to stay there?"

"I have no way of knowing. The female is feeding." She shrugged. "It could be ten minutes. Could be the rest of the day."

"The rest of the day?" Jake snorted. "Well, get them to move."

Shelby turned slowly to face him. "Do what?"

"Get them to move." His tone implied that he was only suggesting the obvious.

"Just how do you propose I do that?"

"I don't know. You're the whale expert here."

Shelby drew a deep breath. Was he trying to provoke her? "That's right, I'm the expert, but we 'whale experts' do not make it our business to scare the whales."

"Fine." Jake's voice betrayed the first raggedness of anger. "I'll take care of it."

"Really?" Shelby asked sweetly. "How?"

"How?"

"That's right. How are you going to scare a forty-ton whale, Captain Lawson? Threaten to sue her?"

"I'll run the boat at her," he said confidently. "She'll get out of the way."

"You do that!" Shelby snapped. "Go right ahead, because as soon as I report that you were out here deliberately trying to run down a nursing mother, your little treasure hunt will be over."

"Run a . . . You know I wouldn't do that. I'm just—"

"Oh, wouldn't you?"

Shelby realized they were both shouting. The crew had casually drifted within earshot, and out of the corner of her eye Shelby noticed Greg and J.B. whispering and watching them like spectators at a prize fight.

"Listen to me, Ms Haynes." Jake was struggling to keep his voice low. "I'm spending a thousand dollars a day on this salvage operation, and I refuse to hold everything up because—" he looked around, noting his crew's rapt attention, and lowered his voice to a terse whisper "—you want to use your position to get back at me for things that...that have nothing to do with this."

"As long as those two whales are in this area, you are not going to proceed. And furthermore, I want that magnetometer cable reeled in." She turned to the fascinated crew members. "Someone please take care of that."

"Nobody move." Jake rapped out the order. He tore his furious gaze from Shelby and turned toward the mother and calf who had resurfaced, now no more than two boat lengths away. "Hey!" he shouted, waving peremptorily at them. "Hey! Get out of here. Scat! Go! Shoo! Go someplace else and eat, damn you!"

A snicker broke from the crew and was quickly stifled. Jake redoubled his shouts.

The bigger whale turned slowly in front of the *Questor* and rolled onto her side to take a clearly bemused look at him.

"I'm afraid it'll take a little more than that to scare her off," Shelby said, torn between anger at his pigheadedness and a desire to giggle uncontrollably.

"All right, I'm asking again. How do you scare a whale?"

"Well, Captain Lawson, that whale is about forty feet long and weighs approximately forty-five tons, and she's not afraid of anything on this planet except...hmm." She made a show of pondering for a moment.

"Except what?"

"Well," Shelby said at last, "you could try painting yourself black and white. She might mistake you for a killer whale. They don't get along, you see."

Jake grinned menacingly. "Underneath it all, you're just a bit of a bureaucrat, aren't you, Ms Haynes?"

Shelby refused to rise to the bait. Instead, she turned toward the crew again. "I would like someone to winch up that magnetometer cable. Now, please. I won't have it tangling or cutting that calf."

"I'm the captain here," Jake said sharply.

"Well?" she challenged.

He glared at her, his face inches from hers, for a long minute. "Marcus!" he shouted at last.

"Yes, sir?"

"Winch up the mag." He nodded at Shelby as she felt the tension of the confrontation manifest itself in the pit of her stomach. "You know," he said in a conversational tone, as though nothing had happened, "you're making my life miserable."

She was startled by the sudden shift in his demeanor. "Am I? I'm . . . sorry."

"You're costing me money, time, the respect of my crew—not to mention the loss of sleep. . . ."

"I'm just trying to—" she began, but he held up a hand.

"No, no, don't apologize again. You see, the funny thing is, I'm starting to enjoy it." He shook his head in bewilderment. "You will let me know when our friends have moved away?"

"Of course," she said to his departing back. As she returned to her charges, she overhead Greg's voice in a loud stage whisper.

"Point goes to Shelby. That's a beer you owe me, J.B."

BY LATE AFTERNOON it was clear she had been right about the whales. Jake sent the crew home in good-natured frustration, muttering something under his breath about "those damned bullheaded whales taking after their guardian."

He'd seemed more relaxed after their confrontation over the mother and calf, as if finally accepting the terms of his uneasy truce with Shelby. Every deliberate lighthearted tease, every shared smile, and she found herself relaxing a little more. Perhaps they would be able to work together after all, despite the complications. If he was going to make the effort, she had to at least try, too.

She arrived home feeling better than she had all week, only to find her answering machine blinking. It was, as she suspected, bad news.

"Hi, Shelby. It's Sam. We've got another. A young bull right whale washed up like the others all the way in Truro. They'll autopsy tomorrow, but it looks like our same mystery illness. Thought I should let you know. Bye. Oh, wait. Call me when you get the chance. I want to hear all about the Great Treasure Hunt. See you."

Shelby sank back in a rattan chair. The news could not have been more depressing. Right whales were among the most endangered of whale species. And at a time when she should be doing something to help them, she was off babysitting Jake.

Well, she would just have to make time for both. She could at least go down to Safeseas after a quick dinner and—

Dinner? Oh, no! Was it tonight?

Please, not tonight, she pleaded silently, running to the kitchen to check the note on her refrigerator door.

It *was* tonight. She had completely forgotten.

Senator Richardson was a political ally of Safeseas, but she had never met him personally, and parties with lots of people she didn't know were not her kind of thing at all—certainly not fresh on the heels of the news she had just received from Sam. But now she was supposed to don her "one nice dress," as Terry had called it, and fly off to spend her evening chitchatting pleasantly with politicos.

She began to feel angry at the imposition but quickly caught herself. She really wasn't being fair. The senator had always been there when Safeseas needed help, and if he'd decided to invite her over to Nantucket, then she should be honored and pleased—or at least act like it.

By six o'clock Shelby was only barely recognizable. She'd pulled her sun-lightened hair into a simple French twist and fastened it with a silver comb, and her grandmother's diamonds glittered at her ears and throat, capturing the slanting rays of an amber sunset. But her black silk dress, which she'd found far back in her closet half-hidden by an enormous stack of *Scientific American*s, was the real coup. It still fit beautifully, revealing just enough to make her feel vaguely sinful.

Cipher looked up at her suspiciously as she maneuvered into high heels and attempted a few unfamiliar steps.

"I know, Cipher. I know," she sighed. "But it's all for a good cause."

She leaned toward the mirror to check her lipstick one last time. Still adjusting to her heels, she took her time descending the back staircase to the yard, half hoping Jake might notice her passing by. But his apartment was dark and his car nowhere in sight.

It was a silly whim, anyway, and a dangerous one, now that they'd finally reached some semblance of a compromise.

Since she was running late and en route to an important rendezvous, the Dodge refused to start, and she was forced, after several minutes of cursing and wheedling, to call a taxi.

Fortunately the cab came promptly. As they drove quickly to the tiny airfield outside Provincetown, she began to feel the first inklings of anticipation. In her rush to get ready, she hadn't really given the evening much thought, and after all, she didn't jet over to Nantucket to dine with senators every day! She was a tad nervous, but the dinner represented an opportunity to do some good for Safeseas. Sure, scientists like herself, and volunteers like Terry, did the work, but politicians arranged for their bills to get paid.

When she arrived at the oversize shed that passed for the airport terminal, only one plane was waiting on the Tarmac: a sleek white Lear jet already warming its twin engines. Shelby jumped out of the cab and ran quickly over to the jet's lowered step-ramp. Peeking inside, she could see the back of the pilot's head outlined by the dim cockpit light.

"Excuse me," she shouted above the engines' ascending whine, "are you my ride to Nantucket?"

Without turning, the pilot motioned her inside. As soon as she had climbed the stairs, the hatch began to close automatically behind her.

"Where do I sit?"

"Right up front here," the pilot muttered, indicating the copilot's seat.

As Shelby made her way toward the cabin, an electric tingle rocketed up her spine.

A tuxedo? What kind of pilot wore a tuxedo?

She'd know those shoulders anywhere.

"Jake!"

"Surprise." He grinned.

"What . . . what are you doing here?" Shelby sputtered, settling into the comfortable leather seat next to him.

"Why, flying us over to Paul's place," he answered with little-boy innocence.

"Paul's place?"

"Senator Richardson to you. He's an old friend. We were at Fort Benning together. A pair of fresh-scrubbed second lieutenants."

Shelby's mind whirled. Jake, an "old friend" of the senator's? "Why didn't you tell me you were going to be at this affair?" she demanded, carefully attempting to cover the expanse of thigh her dress seemed determined to expose.

"Why should I? You didn't tell me."

He did have a point, Shelby realized. But she had the convenient excuse of having completely forgotten about it.

"Besides," Jake continued, "I was afraid if you knew I was going you might not come, and Paul specifically wanted to meet you." He released the brake, and the jet taxied slowly toward the runway. "Also, I need a date."

"A date?"

"Sure. How do you think it would look if the two of us showed up stag? People would think we don't like each other."

"Since when has that been a concern?"

Jake grinned tolerantly and spoke into his headset to the control tower.

"Seat belt on," he instructed, pointing to Shelby's lap. "By the way, nice dress." His gaze grazed her thigh appreciatively. "Very nice."

A flush spread over the skin bared by the low scoop of her neckline. "Are you sure to know how to fly this thing?" she asked hoarsely, trying to make herself heard over the scream of the engines.

"Trust me."

"Famous last words." While he radioed for final permission to take off, Shelby wondered silently why it was that some men looked so absolutely magnificent in a tuxedo. Jake definitely was one of them—the elegant lines of his jacket subtly accentuating his muscular frame, the crisp white collar of his pleated shirt a sharp contrast to his sun-darkened profile. He made an altogether stunning picture, particularly after the bedraggled cutoffs she had grown used to seeing him wear.

On second thought, they had their own special charms.

"Ready?" Jake turned to ask before she had a chance to redirect her gaze.

"As I'll ever be." She nodded, cheeks blazing.

They eased forward toward a runway marked by a series of blue lights, eerily lovely in the velvet black of night. Slowly at first, then faster and faster, they sped along the Tarmac until the lights were a long blue blur and the engines were screaming at full volume. Suddenly Shelby felt the lack of vibration, the sudden pressure of her back against her seat that signaled that they were airborne. Jake pulled back on the yoke, and they soared skyward.

"Not bad for my first try, eh?" Jake joked, easing back into his seat.

"I'll let you know when my stomach catches up with us."

"You're not feeling queasy, are you?" Jake reached across to caress her shoulder reassuringly.

"Oh, no. I've had so many rough days on the water that my insides are cast-iron. It's just such a rush of adrenaline taking off."

"I know." He nodded in agreement. "I'm an addict. I might have been a real pilot if my first love weren't the sea."

They flew in silence for the next few minutes, Jake quietly absorbed in the instrument panel, Shelby trying in vain to construct a mental map of Cap Cod from the faintly glimmering panorama below her.

"Wait a minute," Shelby said. "Aren't we heading the wrong way?"

"Yeah. I thought I'd fly over the site," Jake admitted sheepishly. "It's crazy, but I feel a little strange being away from the *Questor* like this. Like a new mother dropping off her kid at the baby-sitter's."

"But you leave the boat every night," Shelby reminded him.

"Actually I've been spending a little more time on board lately. I don't want any more mysterious fires or equipment breakdowns." He looked at her challengingly. "I don't suppose you've noticed I've been getting in a little later."

Shelby turned away quickly, looking out the window. "No. I haven't noticed. I'm not usually up that late."

"How late?" Jake grinned triumphantly.

"I meant—" Shelby began.

"I know just what you meant." Jake's smile widened even further. "There she is. Just off your side."

Shelby peered out of the window, pressing against the glass for a better angle. "Those lights down there?"

"Yep."

"How can you tell that's the *Questor*? It's just a couple of lights."

"How can a mother recognize her baby's crying in the middle of a crowded nursery?" he answered, not entirely unserious. "Okay. I've tucked her in." He continued the analogy. "Now off to the ball."

Fifteen minutes later they had begun their descent.

The landing was smooth and professional. No sooner had they rolled to a stop and opened the jet's hatch than she saw what seemed to be a mile-long blue-black limousine pull up before them and a uniformed chauffeur step out onto the Tarmac.

Well, of course, she thought, there *would* have to be a limousine. She turned to Jake as they were bowed inside the plush leather interior.

"You know, I'll say one thing for you, Captain Lawson. You certainly know how to travel in style."

# 8

THE RICHARDSON HOME WAS less ostentatious than Shelby had expected, in keeping with the understated Nantucket style. Set atop a rise overlooking Nantucket Sound, the huge, gray-shingled house was surrounded on all sides by unspoiled dunes.

To Shelby's surprise, they were met at the door by the senator himself, a man of Jake's age, prematurely graying at the temples, his dinner jacket open to reveal a considerable paunch beneath his cummerbund.

"Jake Lawson, you old salt!" he cried, clutching Jake's hand in a vigorous handshake. "And who have we here?" He grinned widely at Shelby, leading them into a wide entranceway lined with thick Oriental carpets.

"Paul, meet Shelby Haynes," Jake said, gently wrapping his arm around her waist. "Shelby, this is Paul Richardson, my old—"

"Partner in crime," Richardson finished. "Jake and I used to chase the ladies together, back in our rowdier days—before I got to be so responsible." Richardson signaled a waiter carrying a silver tray laden with champagne glasses. "Of course, I was a sprinter, while Jake here was the distance man." With a wave of his hand he proffered the champagne.

"I'll have to pass," Jake said, "I'm flying. But if you have some of that overpriced foreign soda water..."

Richardson winked conspiratorially. "Sure I do. That's what I have in my glass. A smart politician doesn't get tipsy around potential campaign contributors. I might lose my head and say something blunt. Fred—" he turned to the waiter "—another like mine for my boy Jake here. And Ms Haynes?"

"I'll have the same," Shelby said.

Richardson shepherded them into a cavernous living room that opened onto a verandah overlooking the sea. Elegantly attired men and women milled around the room, starkly outlined against the winter-white carpet and furniture.

Shelby sipped her drink, smiling as the dry bubbles tickled her throat, and listened in silence as Jake and Richardson reminisced. Here in person, the senator seemed a bit less the high-minded politician she'd envisioned, as he and Jake kidded each other like a couple of high-school boys.

At length Richardson directed the conversation to her. "So," he began, "you're the young lady who's supposed to keep our friend Jake here in line. You know, I backed you whale folks one hundred percent. Of course, Jake pulled the old end run around us, anyway."

Jake shook his head good-naturedly and sipped his drink, watching Shelby closely.

"So tell me," Richardson continued, "is Jake minding his manners and being a good boy?"

"Oh—" she hesitated a moment before answering "—I still have to keep my eye on him."

"Yes," said the senator, adding, "and if I know Jake, he's keeping his eye on you, too."

They wandered the room, the senator making long-winded introductions. It quickly became clear that Jake was the center of attraction, an adventurer in the midst of middle-of-the-road politicians and balding businessmen. Shelby knew there were few people in the room who weren't at least a little envious of Jake's life. And she was certain she caught more than a few women admiring his physique while engaging in a bit of dreamy speculation.

Eventually the dinner bell rang, and the guests filed into a lavishly set dining room. Twin crystal chandeliers twinkled like stars over a huge table laden with exquisite arrangements of wildflowers native to the island. Shelby was relieved to find herself seated next to someone with whom she had at least a passing acquaintance. Tim Murphy was the somewhat intense, handsomely graying president of Cape Cod Industries, the manufacturer that had been generous in its opposition to Jake's proposed hunt for the *Evangeline*, supplying legal and financial help.

Shelby was not naive. She'd assumed all along that CCI's efforts had been part of some image-building plan for the company, but still, an ally was an ally, and at least Murphy was a pleasant enough conversationalist.

Jake was seated near the foot of the table, next to the senator's attractive young wife, Elyse. Through most of dinner, Tim Murphy made small talk about Shelby's work, often displaying a surprising knowledge about the area of the search. But as coffee was served with a dessert of sabayon and raspberries, the senator prevailed on a somewhat reluctant Jake to tell the story of the *Evangeline*.

"Come on, Jake. Out with it," Richardson said. "You either tell us about old One-Arm Willy, or I'll have to get up and give an old campaign speech or something."

Despite his hesitation, Jake soon had all eyes on him, and even Shelby, who had heard parts of the story, found herself grudgingly fascinated.

"William Seth Curry," Jake began, "was a privateer, a sort of legal pirate commissioned by the king to prey on enemy ships, or even on other pirates. In Curry's case, it was the French first, and later, when he had worked his way up to his own eight-gun sloop, he took on the pirates who were terrorizing the whole east coast of America.

"It was around 1702, during a provisioning trip ashore on the Cape, that he met the young Charity Stethem. Willy still had two good arms then, and was not a bad-looking fellow. Young Charity was evidently quite bowled over. One thing led to another, as those things will—" Jake smiled engagingly "—and Curry proposed that Charity come away with him. Well, it seems Charity didn't fancy life on a crowded, rat-infested ship and wanted something more stable than life with a common privateer."

Shelby felt a warning tingle and looked across the table to meet Jake's suddenly serious gaze. For a moment the flow of his words was interrupted.

He broke the spell by tasting the coffee that had been freshly poured for him. "Excellent," he pronounced. "Anyway, for his part, Willy didn't much like the notion of giving up a freewheeling life on the sea to become a respectable Cape Cod farmer. He still had dreams of something more . . . stories of Spanish treasure ships and their untold wealth. He swore to Charity he would return in two years' time, when he'd tired of the sea, and settle down with her.

"Unfortunately some time later, Willy made the mistake of running across a French navy ship which, in the process of nearly sinking him, took off his arm with a well-placed cannon shot.

"That more or less convinced him that piracy could be hazardous to his health, and he headed back to the Cape to be reunited with Charity. The two years had passed, and Charity had spent her days searching for a sign of her lover. Since his departure she'd found life without him dull, I suppose. Rain or snow, she went to a little lean-to on the bluffs and waited.

"One morning she was trapped there by a sudden storm. Off in the distance, she could just glimpse the masts of the *Evangeline*, dwarfed by the swells."

Jake sighed heavily, a sound echoed around the table.

"Three times the *Evangeline* rose into view, but there never was a fourth time. Charity waited for two days while the storm continued to rage, and at the end of the second day, the townspeople found her wandering the beach, mad with grief and nearly dead. They tried to take her away, but she resisted. 'I must watch for him,' she said. 'I will watch . . . forever.' Those were her last words. And so—" there was a mischievous twinkle in Jake's eyes "—she still waits and watches . . . a pale ghost haunting the bluff above the beach."

Silence fell on the dining room, as the image lingered in the air before them.

"And what about the treasure?" Richardson broke the collective reverie.

"Well, pirates were often surprisingly detailed in their accounting, since treasure was shared property of the entire crew. We know of emeralds, sapphires, diamonds, silver bracelets, gold chain, etcetera, etcetera. . . ." He waved a hand airily. "But the real treasure is the silver bars and gold ingots that Curry took off a Spanish ship near Havana."

"So what's it worth, Jake? Don't be shy about it," Mrs. Richardson teased.

"That's hard to say exactly. We may find only part of the treasure, and the market value of the jewelry's hard to pin down, but . . . we figure anywhere from one to three."

"One to three what?" Shelby burst out.

Jake favored her with a look of surprised amusement. "One to three hundred million dollars."

The number resonated in the dead silence. Even among the very well-heeled crowd, the figure was astonishing. To Shelby, it was inconceivable.

"Of course, with twenty-five percent to the state and another twenty-five to Washington to pay Paul's phone bill, plus fifty percent of what's left to the crew..." He looked away, seemingly embarrassed.

"So," an attorney from Boston interjected with bright humor, "if you ever need a good lawyer, Captain Lawson—"

Appreciative laughter met his remark. Jake held up a cautioning hand.

"I still have to find the treasure, preferably by the end of the summer. The work gets almost impossible this far north in winter, and there are always delays of one kind or another."

Shelby colored as every head at the table turned to glare at her.

"No, no." Jake laughed. "That's not what I meant. Shelby—Ms Haynes, I mean, has been—"

"Please, Captain Lawson," Shelby interrupted, her voice subtly tinged with frost, "I can defend myself. It's my job," she told the guests, "to make sure that Captain Lawson's search doesn't damage the marine life on Stellwagen Bank. We're in the midst of a still-unexplained epidemic that is killing large numbers of whales. Until we solve that big threat, we at least want to be able to limit the relatively minor threats, like Captain Lawson's treasure hunt."

A quick glance around the table showed more sympathy and agreement than she had expected. Jake's cause seemed so riveting, and her own somehow dull. She felt like the wet blanket, but the senator gave her an encouraging wink, and for the first time that evening Tim Murphy spoke up.

"Well, as you know, we at CCI backed your opposition to the salvage—with all due respect to you, Captain Lawson."

His nod was acknowledged pleasantly by Jake.

"We felt," Murphy continued, "it was of primary importance to protect this young lady's precious charges. May I ask what progress you've made on your mysterious disease?"

"Not much," Shelby admitted. "We autopsy the dead whales, try to save the beached ones that are still alive and keep collating all the data we can get."

"I suppose there must be any number of entirely natural causes for the deaths?"

"There are, yes. Shellfish toxin was our first suspect, but we've eliminated most of those."

Murphy smiled a thin smile. "Well, perhaps between the, uh, disease, and Captain Lawson's...disruption, the whales will decide to move on to less troubled waters."

"That isn't likely," Shelby said resolutely. "I'm afraid it's going to be up to us. Your company was so generous in helping us fight Captain Lawson...perhaps CCI would like to help us further with regular contributions."

"We didn't intend for you to reach an accommodation with Captain Lawson," Murphy said sharply, "we intended to keep him away from Stellwagen Bank." Then, realizing he sounded rude, he softened his tone. "To help protect the whales there, naturally. And although we have spent all we can afford to contribute to charitable causes, we at CCI do wish you luck, Ms Haynes."

"Ms Haynes doesn't need luck," Jake interjected. "She's got guts and determination. And she's right." He nodded thoughtfully. "I'm just an interloper, and a pretty insignificant one at that."

Shelby smiled, warmed by Jake's defense. Seeing him here, dressed in black tie, holding center stage among his economic peers, it was strange how unchanged he was from the man in faded cutoffs trading stories with Marcus or teasing J.B.

Her smile was reflected in his black eyes. "Today," Jake continued, his gaze still locked on hers, "I tried to scare off one of Shelby's whales. I can tell you, although it's unscientific, I would swear that big creature was laughing at me." He chuckled ruefully. "She put me in my place."

"She?" the senator's wife asked, eyebrows raised. "Do you mean she the whale, or—" she inclined her head toward Shelby "—*she*?"

In the general laughter that followed, Shelby never heard his response.

AFTER DINNER the party broke into small groups. Shelby was in the library, chatting with one of the senator's aides, when she heard Jake's voice in the hall.

He appeared suddenly in the doorway, making a show of checking his watch. "No, we're going to have to run. Shelby's got some other commitments. We really should be shoving off. But listen, why don't you and Elyse come out to the *Questor* for lunch—say, next Thursday? Maybe we'll get lucky and have something shiny to show you."

"You know, I might just do that. We're out of session, and hell, it's my vacation. But I don't know about Elyse. She's not big on boats."

"Okay, then see if Tim Murphy will come. That guy doesn't seem to care much for me. Maybe if he had a look-see, he would change his mind."

"I'll run it by him and give you a call." The senator gave his friend a thoughtful look. "Does seem to hold a grudge, doesn't he?"

"Well, nobody likes to lose," Jake said agreeably.

He took Shelby's arm, and together they made their farewells.

"What are these other commitments I'm supposed to have?" Shelby whispered as he guided her toward the door.

"The commitment to get me out of here." Jake paused to pluck a white rose from a vase in the foyer, presenting it to her with a flourish. "Plus whatever other commitments I can talk you into."

TWENTY MINUTES LATER they were airborne. Shelby relaxed in her seat and kicked off her glossy black pumps to rub her feet.

"Well, I survived," she told Jake, giddy with relief, brandy and the exhilarating motion of the jet, flying just below a tight knot of clouds.

"Survived? Are you crazy? You knocked 'em dead."

"May I take off my seat belt now?"

"Sure, until we start to descend."

Stretching, she leaned back in her seat and propped her legs above the instrument panel. "I hate to admit it, but I had fun. I hope I didn't sound like too much of a whale nut."

"You sounded wonderful," Jake replied roughly.

She watched him as he made adjustments to his instruments and removed his headset. With one swift move he swiveled his seat in her direction and reached across to her outstretched legs.

"But the plane!" she cried in mock terror.

"Autopilot," he murmured, stroking the long sweep of her silken leg all the way to her toes.

Gently he swung her toward him until her feet were positioned atop his knees, and began kneading her right foot.

Shelby hadn't realized the price she had paid for wearing the constricting pumps until she felt the steady pressure of

Jake's fingers along the sensitive arch of her foot. "Oh," she moaned contentedly, "you have no idea how delicious that feels."

"Have you ever heard of shiatsu?" His efforts were now focused on her toes, each receiving in turn his undivided attention.

"No—" she smiled "—but I think I've ordered it in a Japanese restaurant by accident. Listen, I hate to be so forward, but may I remind you that I have another foot which is now in comparative agony?"

"Don't worry." He ran his thumbs along the aching base of her heel, and she sighed with delight. "I've made an exhaustive survey of your anatomy." He loosened his tie and the first stud of his shirt to reveal a few dark spirals of hair sprinkled over smooth flesh.

Funny how such a simple, unconscious action could be so devastatingly sexy, she thought.

"Anyway," Jake continued, easing his fingers along the sensitive bones on top of her foot, "shiatsu is an Oriental massage discipline which says that each portion of your foot corresponds to another part of your body. I rub here—" she felt his thumbs increase their pressure "—and I increase the flow of blood to your liver, for example."

"Funny, my liver is feeling awfully relaxed," she teased. "Where, may I ask, did you acquire this fount of knowledge? Are you hiding a geisha down in your apartment?"

"I spent a little time in the Far East chasing down a rumor of a sunken junk loaded with an empress's dowry of jade. Turned out to be a wild-goose chase, but I had a good time." He focused pressure on a quarter-size circle of her foot. "Now this is your neck."

"That is awfully tender," she murmured, closing her eyes to savor the pleasure.

"You must be tense up there."

"I've always been a little stiff-necked," she joked lazily.

"Oh?" Jake said with an affectionate smile. "I hadn't noticed." He moved his sweetly agonizing pressure to another spot. "Now this is your lower back."

"Mmm."

"This is your gall bladder. And *this*—" his eyes caught her own heavy-lidded gaze "—this is your heart."

"That feels especially good." Her voice was deep and dreamy.

He began to knead a new and neglected part of her sole with great seriousness of purpose.

"That," she cooed, "is heavenly. What part of my body is that?"

He looked up with a secret smile and didn't answer.

THEY DROVE HOME from the airport in silence, their relaxed, sexy bantering replaced by unspoken longing so volatile that neither of them trusted speech any longer.

Jake negotiated the lightless road with calculated efficiency and only a grudging respect for the speed limit, the elegant lines of his jaw defined by the pale luminescence of the dashboard lights.

Shelby knew there would be no turning back tonight, no last-minute changes of heart. She allowed herself a brief glance in Jake's direction, then looked away again toward the dark winding road ahead.

It occurred to her in an instant flicker of recognition that she had just seen the choice unfold before her: the absolute certainty of Jake, here, tonight; followed by a road for which there were no maps, no guideposts, no guarantees.

Jake was right. Sometimes there were risks worth taking.

He parked the car in front of the house and turned to her. Even in the dark interior she could see his eyes interrogating her, waiting for an answer to the question that still separated them.

Words caught in her throat like cotton. Silently she reached into her bag and retrieved the key to her apartment. Lifting his right hand from the steering wheel, she dropped the key into his palm and closed his long fingers around the shiny metal.

He said nothing, but she heard the unsteady rhythm of his breathing as he climbed out and walked around to open her car door. He took her hand, assisting her out with a firm, assured grip, and led her through the gate and across the lawn, right hand pressed against the small of her back. Wordlessly they climbed the steps to the second floor. She watched in veiled amusement as he fumbled with the key to her door, muttering an exasperated expletive under his breath.

When at last they entered her apartment, they were greeted with exuberant excess by Cipher.

"Hello, boy." Jake gave the dog a perfunctory pat.

"Three's a crowd, Cipher," Shelby told him, holding open the door so he could make an extended trip to the fenced-in yard.

She closed the door in his wake and took a deep, steadying breath. "Now," she said, suddenly overcome with shyness, "can I get you anything? A brandy? A stale Twinkie?"

"You know what I want, Shelby," he said quietly.

She took his hand tentatively. "Come on. I'll give you the royal tour. This," she said in a reedy voice not in the least resembling her own, "is the living room...."

"Shelby."

"Yes?"

"I've seen your apartment."

"Oh." She stopped in confusion. Taking a deep breath, she led him into the hallway. "Well, then I guess you know that this is my bedroom."

Entering slowly, she absently flicked on her bedside-table lamp, the soft glow dispersing the shadows. "Um," she began, "I guess we really won't be needing that...." She reached to extinguish the light, but Jake captured her wrist in his powerful hand.

"No," he whispered firmly. "Tonight I want to see you, Shelby. Every glorious inch of you."

His white-hot stare melted her down to the bone. "I suspect," she tried to tease, "you've seen plenty of women in your time, Captain Lawson."

"I've never seen *you*," he said, his voice quietly insistent but tinged with mischief. He brought her hand to his lips and caressed it with a breeze-soft kiss. "Here. Let me show you."

The huskiness in his voice belied the deliberate slowness of his movements as he drew her to the full-length mirror on her wall.

Before her in the mirror stood a woman flushed with readiness like a ripe peach, her eyes dewy, her lips half-parted. Shelby liked what she saw: a passionate woman, a beautiful woman.

Behind her Jake towered, hands clasping her bare shoulders possessively. "See, love?" she heard his whispered question. "Do you see now why I want you so?"

Her hair cascaded around her shoulders as he removed her silver comb. "Much better," he said, lacing his fingers through the soft blond strands.

She watched, transfixed, as he cupped a breast, her breast, coaxing her sensitive nipple to proud firmness beneath the black silk.

"This damned dress," he murmured, "has been driving me crazy all night."

His fingers tormented her through the slinky barrier, all sensation rippling outward from that single, tiny summit. She stood perfectly still, a shimmering silver mirage in her old mirror, allowing—silently begging—Jake to slide the spaghetti-thin straps of her dress from her shoulders, mesmerized as the black silk glided over the gentle slopes of her breasts.

"Look, darling..." Jake's breath was ragged as he cradled her fullness in his palms.

Was it his heart pounding frantically in her ears, or her own? As she gently undulated her hips, the dress slipped from her and fell to the floor. She stood revealed, but for the flimsy protection of her black lace panties.

Jake reluctantly released his hold on one captive globe, letting his hand slide down the petal-soft expanse of Shelby's abdomen. He toyed playfully with the lacy edge riding high on her hip, watching her eyes widen in the mirror and then flutter and slowly close. Beneath his left hand, still softly kneading one firm, impossibly smooth breast, he could feel the breathless syncopation of her heart. Now; he had to ask her now, before he lost what little self-control he had left.

"Shelby, are you sure?" His voice was hoarse, coming to him through a fog of passion so thick it threatened to blind him to everything but his absolute need.

"Please." Her voice, sweetly plaintive, wrapped around his heart and clutched it. "Please, Jake."

She turned to face him, and he crushed her to his chest while his hands roamed the tawny smoothness of her back, reflected still in the soft glow of the mirror.

"I want you, Jake," she whispered. "I want you to make love to me."

The words set him on fire. He heard her whimper as he knelt and slipped her panties off. Catching her in his arms, he lifted her effortlessly from the floor and in two great strides carried her to the bed. He stepped back to savor the sight, the heart-stopping loveliness of her.

Shrugging off his tuxedo coat, he dropped it indifferently to the floor, consciously slowing his pace to stem the tide of his arousal, and began unfastening the tiny studs of his pleated shirt.

He looked up to see Shelby's misted gray eyes drinking him in, a small smile gracing her moistened lips.

"Don't stop now," she crooned.

"Ah . . . is this okay?"

"Just perfect."

"No." Jake smiled. "I meant, are you protected?"

"Oh." Shelby nodded. "Yes, I'm taking the Pill."

"Maybe we should turn out the light," he suggested, feigning modesty.

"You should have thought of that. Too late now. Besides," she parodied him coyly, "I want to see every inch of you."

Without a word Jake unfastened his cuff links, tossing them carelessly onto the nightstand and yanking at the tails of his shirt until they came free. He pulled first at one arm, then the other, and let the shirt fall atop his crumpled jacket.

He hadn't taken his gaze from her, watching her expression become less detached, less restrained, less and less controlled, until her eyes glittered in reflection of his own diamond-hard hunger. He had to touch her, or he would burn alive.

Within moments he was free of his remaining clothing and lowering himself beside her, the cool sheets doing nothing to moderate the heat of his flesh. The feel of her skin, the taste of her mouth, the scent of her arousal were necessities as absolute as air, more precious than gold.

Shelby welcomed him to her, grateful for the hard heat of his body pressed against the length of her own. Her fingertips raked his shoulders, journeyed to feel the urgent pulse in his neck, marveled at the harsh bristle of his jaw. Her nails made a soft rasping sound as she drew them down his cheek.

Brushing the ridges and sinews of his chest with her mouth, she savored the salty taste of his skin and the faint, fresh scent of soap. His chest rose and fell quickly, and she felt his self-control weaken as he gripped her by the arms and pressed her back against the mattress, adamant in his need to taste her, to touch her.

Traveling the soft underside of her breasts, he planted kisses on the long shallow of her ribs and sent exquisite tremors shimmering downward. She felt his lips on the rounded ridges of her pelvis.

"Jake," she groaned, "I want you inside me." Her voice was tortured with longing. "Please, no more. Don't make me wait," she whispered. "Please, don't make me wait."

"I won't make you wait, love," he promised. "I'll make you want to wait."

Shelby felt him move beyond her touch until his hot breath tickled her inner thighs. Tenderly he pressed her legs apart and steadied her hips with his hands as he began to weave a sublime, magic spell. Again and again he coaxed her to the very edge of a sparkling vortex, until, after an eternity, she pulled him to her.

"Now," she begged, voice quaking, "I need you now."

"I need *you*, Shelby," Jake whispered.

He entered her slowly, with a soft groan, then paused when she had taken him fully. His stillness was tantalizing agony. She began a slow rotation of her hips beneath him, entreating him, grasping his hard buttocks with desperate hands.

Then, yielding at last to his own desire, he began to thrust into her urgently, his breath coming quickly, his moans a deep contrast to her own. He cradled her in his arms, carrying her along with him effortlessly as he rocked, and together they found an ancient and perfect rhythm.

Shelby clutched his straining shoulders as the fire in her veins raged out of control. She wanted to tell Jake, to reach him, but somehow she knew he sensed her joy as he transported her to a place beyond doubt, beyond thought, beyond herself.

When she heard Jake groan her name as his own tattered self-control was blown away, lifting her from the bed with the power of his final, magnificent shudder, she knew he had joined her there.

# 9

SHELBY LAY BLANKETED in the radiant heat of Jake's body, riding with him through their last sweet spasms. At last they were both quiet. Their bodies still joined, Jake brought his lips to hers in a long, languorous kiss, as if to seal the secret pact between them. He pulled away from her slowly, rolling onto his side to draw her back against his cooling chest. She fit there perfectly, like an egg in a nest, cradled in his strength, listening to the slowing rhythm of his heart.

"Don't ever move," she warned him, reveling in her body's wondrous exhaustion.

"Don't worry. I have no intention of ever moving." His arms enfolded her even more tightly.

She sighed rapturously and ran her toes along his bristly, hard calf.

Jake nuzzled her neck and caressed the flushed swell of her breast with infinitely gentle fingers. A little shudder echoed through her as she watched his hand snake seductively toward the moist tangle between her legs. She twisted her head to face him and found eyes still smoldering and the devilish hint of a smile.

"I thought you weren't going to move," she protested weakly, moaning in response to his fluttering fingertips.

"I'm barely lifting a finger," Jake responded, trapping her in his grip as she tried to wriggle free. He continued his playful exploration.

"I'm . . ." she gasped, feeling evidence of his renewed desire pressed against her. She was melting again, plunging back into the shimmering ocean of sensation that beckoned. "I'm..." she began again, struggling for breath. "Oh, Jake, I'm . . . getting awfully weak on willpower."

"That's the whole idea."

Suddenly she felt his head jerk up, and a chill slap of air assailed her as he pulled away.

"What was that?" he asked.

From the living room came the sound of someone banging on the screen door.

"Who on earth can that be?" Shelby wondered. "It's still dark out."

"I'll get it." Jake pulled on his pants and headed, shirtless, to the door. Shelby followed in her robe.

Jake flicked on the outside light and opened the door to reveal Greg and Janine.

"Captain," Greg began breathlessly. "We looked for you downstairs, and when you weren't there, Jan thought Shelby might know—"

"Come in, come in," Jake said, laughing. "No harm done."

They entered tentatively, watching Jake for cues. "Please sit down," Shelby told them, her vague embarrassment overshadowed by concern at their darkly anxious expressions. "Would anyone like coffee?"

"Don't go to any trouble, Shelby," Janine told her, "and please accept our humble apologies for barging in on you two like this. I'm afraid we've had some trouble with the *Questor*."

"What now?" Jake demanded.

"We got a call from the Coast Guard at the hotel about half an hour ago," Greg explained. "J.B. and Thomas were doing night duty on board, and when they woke up, they found themselves about thirty-five miles from where we dropped anchor."

"What the hell?" Jake growled.

"The anchor line was cut," Janine explained, sighing. "Clean through. J.B. radioed the Coast Guard and asked them to try to reach you. Tom and J.B. are bringing her back in now. They estimate they'll be back here around eight."

"I don't suppose you have a spare anchor lying around, Captain?" Greg tried to joke.

Jake ignored him. "J.B. and Tom on board, not...anyone else?"

Greg nodded. "Just them."

As Shelby listened intently from the kitchen, she turned to find that Janine had joined her.

"Need any help in here?" Janine asked.

"Oh, no. Just waiting for the machine here to quit dripping."

"Shelby," Janine began, somewhat hesitantly, "I just wanted to tell you how happy I am about you and Jake."

"Why, thanks," she responded, warmed by Janine's sincere smile.

"In all the time I've known Jake," Janine said softly, "I've never seen him as happy—as alive, somehow—as he's been since we fished you up out of the sea that day."

From the other room, as though to deny her words, they heard Jake's voice, quietly angry. They both grinned, despite themselves.

Janine shrugged. "Even with all this mess, he's happy. Believe me, normally he'd be twice as mad. Here," she said, taking hold of a serving tray, "let me help you with that."

They returned to the living room where Jake and Greg sat in gloomy contemplation.

"I just don't like the look of it." Jake sighed at last, accepting a steaming mug from Shelby. "Thanks," he said, fingers lingering on her hand.

"Neither do I, Captain," Greg agreed. "A few problems, a few gremlins . . . well, that's to be expected, but this is beginning to look like someone is out to get us."

Jake nodded sadly. "Yeah. I haven't wanted to start thinking that way."

"Well, I still don't," Janine said firmly. "We shouldn't let a little bad luck get us all paranoid."

"A *lot* of bad luck," her fiancé countered.

"But you're suggesting one of us, one of the crew, is deliberately sabotaging the salvage. I just can't believe that."

"Maybe it's the ghost of One-Arm Willy trying to keep us from his gold," Jake said in a tone that was only half-joking. "But one thing we can do is bring the *Questor* in to pick up a new anchor, and while she's in, go over every piece of equipment. Replace anything that looks even slightly worn. I want to know everything is in A1 condition. That way, if something goes wrong again . . . well, let's just hope it doesn't. And, Greg, I want two people on every task."

"To check up on each other," Greg said coolly.

"Call it quality control."

"Sure, Captain." His resentment at being treated as a possible suspect was obvious, and even Janine looked unusually somber as they turned to leave.

When the door had shut behind the departing couple, Jake slumped onto the couch, looking pensive and a little dejected as he stared into the empty space and toyed with his mustache. Shelby joined him, nestling her head against his bare chest.

"Well, I guess this tears it. We have a definite problem. I've suspected it for some time," he murmured slowly, "but I've been too damn stubborn to admit the problem's in my own backyard."

"What do you mean?"

"I've been so loyal, so blindly loyal, to my crew that I've refused to accept the fact that we have a saboteur on board. But I can't keep hiding my head in the sand."

"But who?" Shelby asked guardedly. "Why?"

"If I knew that, we'd still have an anchor." He chuckled dryly. "Possibly it's someone working for another salvager who wants to get his hands on the *Evangeline* treasure."

"You could go to the police, tell them what's happened."

"No." Jake shook his head. "They'll drag everyone in for questioning, destroying what's left of morale in the process, and I'll lose half the summer when we could have been digging. Not to mention the fact that whoever's doing this is no fool. Chances are he wouldn't be careless enough to be caught. And then what? Back to work with everyone watching everyone else day and night? It would mean the end."

"But this could be dangerous, Jake." Shelby gripped his hand in her own with fierce tenderness.

"I'm not going out looking for trouble, but I'm not letting anyone scare me off, either. What if what happened with your tanks is part of this, too? It's long past time I got to the bottom of this," he said resolutely. Suddenly his eyes brightened. "You know, I think I'd better have a look at the situation myself. Everything else that has happened could have been done by someone on board—the breakdowns, the magnetometer cable, even the fire—but cutting your own anchor line and drifting around without power in the middle of busy sea-lanes in the dark? That would be plain suicidal. So maybe, just maybe, there's another element to this. Someone in a boat could have drifted up alongside, cut the line. . . . We could have two problems, not one, or—"

"Or what?" Shelby demanded.

"I don't know, but I know one way to find out. I'm just going to pull a little stakeout tonight."

"Not without me, you're not," Shelby said firmly.

"Now look here, my friend. My problems are my own responsibility." He glared at her with such patronizing authority she couldn't help but smile.

"What's so amusing?" he demanded gruffly.

"You, laying down the law. We're on dry land now, Captain, and I make my own rules."

"There is absolutely no way that I am going to let you come along," Jake announced. "No way at all."

*We'll see about that*, Shelby vowed silently. His problems had become hers, too, now, whether Jake wanted to admit it or not.

JAKE ASSISTED SHELBY into the launch and wondered, for the hundredth time that night, how on earth she had managed to talk her way around him.

"Come on, Captain," she urged him in a soft whisper. "What's the problem? Forget your seasick pills?"

He frowned at her in frustration. It was past midnight, and swift-moving clouds had kept the moon at bay for the past few hours. Still, Shelby's eyes seemed to shine with some inner light all her own.

He didn't want her to come. She didn't understand the possibility of danger, or if she did, she wasn't letting on. This was an ugly game they were playing, and he wanted Shelby off the field and safely in the stands, cheerleading and nothing more.

Maybe he could change her mind. No problem: maybe he could move a few mountains before breakfast while he was at it. Shelby was nothing if not strong willed. Still, he had to try. He simply couldn't let anything happen to her.

"Shelby." He hopped into the Zodiac and sat beside her. "I can't let you go tonight." He adopted the authoritarian, no-nonsense voice that sometimes (though not always) worked on his crew. "The truth is, you're just going to be in the way."

"Forget it, Jake. It won't work."

He sighed audibly, opting for his long-suffering-parent routine—which seldom had any effect on his crew. "We're talking about a long, extremely dull night, Shelby."

"Then I'll do my best to liven things up a bit."

Her fingers traveled the inside of his jean-covered thigh with uncomfortably serious consequences. He shifted his weight and captured her hand in his, bringing it to his lips. It was hopeless. He couldn't control this woman, wouldn't be so damned smitten if he could. "All right," he told her. "We'll play it your way."

He cast off, fired up the outboard engine and guided the launch toward the open water. The sea at night was always a surprise—treacherous, vaguely sinister, yet irresistibly bewitching.

"Isn't it glorious?" Shelby called to him as they picked up speed and began a hard dance over choppy waves.

He nodded but didn't speak. Words cluttered his brain at times like this, meaningless distractions. He often felt that way in Shelby's presence: incapable of expressing himself, of telling her how profoundly these past days with her had changed him. As though he had been wandering the world, always searching, one half of a puzzle, struggling to locate the missing piece that would mesh with him, that would make him complete.

Only when making love to her did he feel he'd expressed his feelings. Then he had reached her. He was certain of it. But here, now or tomorrow—who could tell? He felt as though he were navigating by the stars alone, for the first time.

Jake cut the engine to its lowest speed until they were creeping along slowly, almost silently but for the low-pitched throbbing sound.

"We're getting close," he answered Shelby's quizzical look. "We should try to be as quiet as possible from here on in. Sound carries all too well on an empty sea."

They peered expectantly ahead into the dark, until at last Jake was able to make out the darker-than-night profile of the *Questor* and the lonely glow of her mooring lights. No light shone from the cabin or the deck.

"Good," he whispered, "they've gone to bed." He killed the engine and slipped the launch's anchor as silently as possible into the inky water. Three hundred yards away J.B. and Thomas would be snoring in their bunks, unaware that they were being watched. The thought made Jake uneasy. Here he was, distrusting two young kids who practically idolized him.

"I feel like a damned spy sneaking around out here like this," he whispered sourly.

"Don't," Shelby hushed him. "Those two and every other honest member of your crew would want you to do whatever you must to protect this expedition. Whoever has been sabotaging this salvage will have no friends."

"Yeah, I know all that," he said. "And I still feel like a jerk." They sat in silence until Jake got up from the bench he was sitting on and went rummaging around in the stores they had brought along.

"We did bring coffee, didn't we?" he asked.

"Yes, Captain. It's in the thermos, behind the cooler."

"Thank goodness. It's likely to be a very long night of looking for nothing."

"What are we looking for, exactly?" Shelby asked curiously.

Jake pursed his lips and gazed toward his boat, riding the gentle swells. "I'm not really sure. Another boat, maybe, although it isn't likely they'd strike two nights in a row." Yes, he thought, another boat, or one of those two nice kids coming out on deck to cut a line or go down into the engine room... No. There might be a traitor on board, but he would swear it was neither of those two. But then, whom *did* he suspect? Who could have been responsible, who among the crew had the opportunity each time—?

"Jake?"

He shook himself, awakening from his unhappy daydream. No point in speculating, he realized—it could have been anyone. He turned to Shelby. "Yes?"

"You seemed to have gone far away. I was getting lonely."

She was smiling up at him from her perch on the bench in the stern. No glum fantasy could stop the answering smile that formed on his own face. Lord, she was beautiful.

"Well, I'm back," he said, chuckling. He dropped onto the bench, wrapping his arm around her. She nestled close, molding her soft curves against him, and an unexpected surge of longing quickened his breath. He caught the faint scent of orange blossoms in Shelby's hair.

"Cold?" he asked.

"Not anymore." They both wore heavy, loose-knit fisherman's sweaters to protect them from the ocean's chill, and he had taken the precaution of bringing along foul-weather gear and heavy blankets, just in case.

"Don't forget we have sandwiches." Shelby nodded toward the Styrofoam cooler. "But be careful. My camera's right on top of the lid. I wouldn't want you to owe me for two cameras."

"Camera? What are you going to shoot out here?"

"Whatever, if anything, happens," she replied. "It's a still camera, loaded with infrared film."

"That was a very good idea," Jake complimented. *One I should have thought of myself*, he added silently.

"Well, I don't have a night scope, so we can't really see what we're photographing, but if it puts off heat, we'll see it in the developed film. Now aren't you glad you insisted I come along?"

"I'll think about it." *Yes, if all goes well*, he thought, *then I'll be glad, but . . .*

They sat quietly watching the *Questor*, the musical splash of the ocean against their fiberglass hull the only sound. Jake lifted his legs to stretch them out on the bench, and Shelby followed suit, sitting between his legs while she leaned back against his chest.

"Jake?" she said softly. "There's something I've been meaning to ask you."

"Are you after my deepest, darkest secrets?" he joked.

"You'd better believe it. But right now I'm just curious about something."

"Shoot."

"Am I on your list of suspects?"

Jake laughed loudly, then, remembering where he was, stifled his mirth. "Why, are you ready to confess?"

"Stop teasing. I'm serious."

He held her to him tightly, silent, as though considering the question seriously. "Well, aside from the practical questions of opportunity, there is the overriding fact of your personality."

"What about my personality?" He could feel the slight tensing of her shoulders but knew instinctively she was only pretending to be concerned.

"Well, love, I think if you wanted to stop me that badly, you might try hauling me into court or pirating my boat or challenging me to a duel at dawn, but sneaking around cutting cables and setting fires . . . no. Not you."

"You sound pretty sure. Maybe I'm just a very clever sneak. I might have even faked the problem with my tanks, just to throw you off."

"You don't have a deceptive bone in your lovely body," Jake scoffed. "You're about as sneaky and underhanded as one of your whales."

"I'm not sure I like that comparison," Shelby complained, but as she snuggled closer against his chest, he knew she wasn't entirely displeased.

"Would you mind a lot if I just kind of dozed off?" she asked, yawning. "Someone kept me up all last night."

"You could have turned in early tonight," Jake countered.

"Oh, so that was your plan. It was all just a ploy to get me out of the way."

"Guilty." Jake hung his head, feigning remorse. "Are you mad at me now?"

"Furious," she answered dreamily.

"How can I make it up to you?"

Her voice came from the edge of sleep. "I'll dream up something."

# 10

SHELBY AWOKE in the gentle cradle of Jake's arms, the rough wool of his fisherman's sweater tickling her cheek. "Some help I am," she mumbled apologetically.

"Hey," Jake told her, "you kept me nice and warm. Besides, nothing has happened. Zilch."

"What time is it?" She stood and stretched her legs, still tingly from sleep.

"Three a.m."

"I thought stakeouts were supposed to be exciting. They always are on TV."

"Brushing your teeth is exciting on TV," he quipped. "I told you things would be dull."

She reached up and tousled his hair playfully. Safe in his arms like this, everything seemed remarkably simple. As long as she didn't think about the future, these moments together were pure bliss. And she wasn't above a little self-deception, if it meant she could feel this heavenly.

Suddenly a strange sound erupted, geyserlike, not more than twenty feet from their bow.

"Sounds like...someone blew a tire," Jake said with a chuckle.

Shelby clambered up onto the prow, camera in hand. "It's a whale, silly. Humpback, from the sound," she said excitedly. "Very close, too." She aimed her camera in the direction of the sound and snapped the shutter at the moment a huge mottled tail broke the surface.

"Aargh!"

"What's the matter?"

"Just a little whale humor." Shelby laughed. "My jeans are soaked through! He was a big one, though. Probably figures he puts up with enough all day long and wants to be left alone at night." She leaned over the side, speaking in a loud whisper, "All right. If that was you, Harold, I'll get you for this!"

Jake took her hand, helping her down from her precarious perch. "Well, it serves you right." He laughed, relieved that she was all right. "But you'd better get out of those wet pants or you'll get pneumonia."

"That's a likely excuse," she joked. But the breeze was just chilly enough to convince her of the wisdom of his advice.

"Here." He tossed her a blanket. "You can put this on."

She handed him the camera and shucked off her sodden blue jeans and panties, tying the blanket around her waist.

"Smile," Jake ordered.

She looked up to see the lens of her camera pointed at her.

"Oh, no, you don't!" she began, but he had already snapped the picture. "It won't come out, you know," she lied.

"I thought it would pick up anything that gives off heat." He smiled seductively. "You should show up just fine."

She moved to him and pried the camera from his hand, setting it down on the bench. "What am I going to do with you?" she asked with pretended exasperation.

"I've got a few suggestions."

"Oh?" She melted into his waiting arms, kissing his neck, standing on her toes to place a kiss on the corner of his mustache.

In response he lowered himself slowly onto the bench, drawing her down onto his lap.

"Jake...we shouldn't," Shelby managed to gasp out. "Not here."

"No. You're right. We shouldn't," he said, but his hand roamed beneath her sweater, leaving a simmering trail in its wake.

She found his lips with hers, parting them with her tongue. Her fingers twined in his tousled hair, and she loosened her hold on the blanket, which slipped away, forgotten, to the deck.

Slowly he lifted her sweater to the ocean breeze. Her nipples stiffened, and he lowered his mouth to find them, warming them with the liquid caress of his tongue.

"Jake..." she began, meaning to stop him, meaning to say that they couldn't, they shouldn't.... But her hand was already fumbling with the buckle of his belt.

Gently he rose from the bench, one arm carrying her along with easy strength, the other lowering his jeans. Then he settled back, easing her onto him with perfect control.

"Oh," she sighed ecstatically at the first touch of his body, "you feel so wonderful."

She felt herself welcome him, enveloping his powerful need in secret warmth, until at last she rested fully in his lap. Jake's eyes were closed, his hands locked on her hips. As her body teased him with delicate tremors, she could feel his struggle for control, waged in the tense muscles of his neck and shoulders.

She moaned aloud, and Jake brushed a finger against her lips.

"Shh." He smiled, nodding toward the *Questor*. "We'll wake the neighbors."

For a lovely time they rolled with the boat's gentle see-sawing motion.

"Are you cold?" Jake managed to ask through clenched teeth, in a husky echo of his normal voice.

"What do *you* think?" Shelby whispered.

Jake thrust into her more deeply still, rocking her body in his arms until, at the same sublime moment, they exploded, becoming part of the star-strewn sky. With unspoken agreement they remained joined, forgetting time, riding the ocean's gentle swells until the earth turned away from the moon to meet the first gray tendrils of dawn.

At last Shelby reluctantly disengaged herself from Jake's grasp and began pulling on her still-damp clothing. She gazed off toward the rising sun.

"Looks like there may be a front moving in," she commented. "I kind of hope there is. I don't know about you, but I could use an excuse to take a couple of days off and catch up on my sleep."

"A storm?" Jake got to his feet. "This time of year?"

Shelby laughed. "This is New England, not Texas. We have a saying up here—if you don't like the weather, just wait an hour and it'll change."

"Damn." He followed the direction of her gaze. "You know, I think you're right. Well—" he raised his palms in a gesture of acceptance "—I can't do much about the weather.... Except, of course, stay inside—under the covers with someone warm." He took her in his arms. "Any suggestions about the someone?"

"Yes, as a matter of fact. Cipher can warm up a whole bed."

"Cipher? Your dog? I had a slightly different idea...."

"I'm sure you did—" Shelby kissed his chin "—but rain or sleet or snow, my work just piles up, and this little break just means back to the grindstone for me." She turned serious for a moment. "But don't you go off after bad guys without me around."

"Humph," Jake snorted. "My first attempt here at playing detective didn't exactly accomplish anything. A pity to drag you along on this wild-goose chase. Sorry you came?"

She grinned wickedly. "Not at all."

BY THE TIME the sun had risen fully, the threatened storm appeared in earnest. An endless torrent of rain washed down the narrow streets of the town, closing the outdoor cafés and dispersing the tourists. In the harbor gusting winds crowned the waves with white and showered buildings along the wharf with salt spray.

Shelby walked the six blocks from the wharf to Safeseas, leaping puddles and rivulets while fighting the wind for control of her umbrella. Entering the office for what she felt was the first time in ages, it almost seemed like alien territory. She shook out her umbrella and experienced a pang very much like guilt as she surveyed the familiar walls, their flaws and cracks concealed by Greenpeace and Sierra Club posters and yellowing charts of the waters around Cape Cod.

The spell was broken by Dr. Tuan, who appeared suddenly in the doorway to his office, holding a manila folder and peering at her over the top of his glasses.

"What are you doing here?" he asked without preliminary.

"I'm here to work," she answered defensively. She pointed at the folder. "What's that?"

"Toxicology reports." His voice sounded weary, and she noticed that his shirt was rumpled, the front stained with what had to be pizza sauce.

"Have you been working on those all night?" she asked, softening her tone.

The doctor shrugged. "Couldn't sleep, anyway. I drank too much tea."

"Did you find anything new?"

Tuan shook his head dejectedly. "Traces of shellfish toxin, but not nearly enough to cause real trouble. The problem is not knowing what to look for. I'm still leaning toward some new virus, but the possibility of toxin still exists. These tests are only down to the parts per million. We can run them again all the way down to parts per billion, but that means probably three weeks to two months before the lab in Boston can get to us. In the meantime . . ." He let the sentence hang in the air.

"Could be a combination—toxins that weaken the immune system enough to allow your mystery virus to replicate."

"Yes," Tuan agreed, "it could be a lot of things. But I can only cover so many leads at one time."

"Well, New England Aquarium is trying to trace back to elements in the whales' food chain, and they may turn up something. And Wood's Hole Oceanographic is anxious to help if they can get funding." Shelby threw up her hands hopelessly.

"So, in other words, it's up to us." Tuan smiled faintly.

"No." Shelby felt bitterness and guilt well up in her. "No, it's really up to you and your team, Doctor, because I have a week's worth of pencil pushing to catch up on while the storm lasts, and when it clears—" She bit her lip in frustration.

"Ah, yes. The great treasure hunt." Tuan seemed about to say more, but instead, holding up the folder with a rueful expression, withdrew to the sanctuary of his office.

The great treasure hunt.

Tuan understood her frustration; they all did at Safeseas. It wasn't easy, running a vital scientific inquiry with her hands tied behind her back.

But the awful truth was, she was actually enjoying her work on the *Questor*—most of the time, at least. Although Jake was as serious in his hunt for treasure as she was in her hunt for the mystery disease, there was something seductively upbeat about the *Questor*'s mission. It was, after all, a lot of fun. And faced with the grim intensity of her work at Safeseas, it made a refreshing contrast.

The silent admission merely served to double her burden of guilt. She would just have to work twice as hard to atone for all the time she'd lost to the *Questor* oversight.

Then, someday in the far-distant future when all this was behind her, she would catch up on sleep.

BY NOON SHE HAD BARELY made a dent in her paperwork, and the words on the lab report in front of her were beginning to blur. Shelby decided to slip down the street and pick up a sandwich—fortification for the remaining stack of paper overflowing her In basket.

But before breaking for lunch, she might as well develop the film she'd taken the night before during the stakeout. It would be a small victory, but if she could identify the specific whale in the picture, it would be a victory nonetheless.

She entered the tiny darkroom, switching on the panel light outside warning others not to enter. The familiar, acrid smell assaulted her nose, and she paused a moment, allowing her eyes to adjust to the unnatural red glow of the overhead light.

Carefully she began measuring chemicals and methodically laying out her equipment. It never paid to hurry in the darkroom, as she had learned on more than one occasion. Still, it was only a few minutes of well-practiced work before the first exposure began to appear at the bottom of a shallow pan of liquid.

It was not, as she'd hoped, a picture of a whale. The film revealed a partially clothed woman—herself—"heat-producing" areas showing up bright as neon on the infrared film.

"Oh, my God," she muttered. "I'm going to have to remember to burn this before it ends up on the bulletin board."

The second photograph brought a smile to her lips. It clearly showed the upraised tail of a large humpback preparing to dive. In the distance far behind it she could make out the shadow of the *Questor*, fuzzily indistinct.

"Hmm," she commented under her breath. "I hadn't realized we were that far from the *Questor*."

She pulled out a magnifying glass and switched on the white overhead light to get a closer look at the tail markings. Squinting, she found the distinctive notch two-thirds of the way down the left side.

"Ah, Harold. I knew it was you."

"Hey, Shelby, are you here somewhere?"

She heard the voice only faintly but immediately recognized it. Moving to set the photos aside, she hesitated, as though her hand did not want to let it go. Something was tickling the edge of her awareness, but she couldn't quite—

"Shelby, it's Jake. Come out, come out, wherever you are."

She shook her head to drive off the uneasiness and opened the darkroom door.

"Oh, there you are," Jake said, striding to meet her and taking her in his arms. "I ran into Dr. Tuan in front. He said he thought you were still around here somewhere."

"I was in the darkroom," she explained, still feeling distracted.

"Why bother?" Jake laughed. "With those storm clouds out there, it's dark everywhere."

"Is it still raining?"

"I'm afraid so. But speaking of rain and gloom, I have a two-part proposition for you."

"Two-part? That sounds interesting."

"And the first part is, you let me buy you lunch."

"What's the second part?"

"I'll tell you that part over dessert."

Shelby hesitated. She really didn't want to take a long lunch when she had so much work ahead of her, but seeing the excitement in Jake's eyes, she somehow couldn't bear to send him away.

"A quick lunch," she conceded at last. "No dessert."

The storm hadn't let up at all, but walking arm in arm, they managed to keep dry huddled beneath Shelby's umbrella.

As was usual for the little tavern, the Governor Bradford was nearly filled to capacity. Jake found a table in the far corner, and as soon as a waitress arrived on the scene, he ordered a bottle of champagne.

"Oh, Jake, no," Shelby objected. "What I need is coffee," she told the waitress. "The stronger the better."

"Bring both," Jake directed. "One sip won't hurt. Besides, I'm trying to set the stage here."

"For what?" Shelby asked warily, watching the waitress make her way toward the bar. Jake's ebullience only seemed to deepen her own uneasiness. Why was she so edgy?

"Part two of my proposition."

She felt him reach for her right hand. Absently she fingered the hard calluses on his palm. The treasure hunt had left its mark on him in many ways—in the hard definition of his muscles, the dark, even brown of his skin and in the rough caress of his palm that she knew so well...that knew *her* so well.

"Okay," she said, trying to match his light tone, "give me a hint."

The waitress returned with the champagne bottle in a small silver bucket and two fluted glasses. After she'd filled each glass and departed to retrieve Shelby's coffee, Jake lifted his glass in a toast.

"Just a sip. You promised," he chided.

Shelby dutifully raised her glass.

"To . . ." Jake paused dramatically, considering his options.

"My arm is getting tired."

Jake rolled his eyes. "Oh, all right, then. To the islands."

She met his gaze uncertainly. "Which islands?"

"That's entirely up to you. Pick an island, any island."

"Alcatraz."

Jake sighed tolerantly. "Ah, you incurable romantic, you. I had something a tad more exotic in mind—say Antigua, Martinique, Barbados?"

Shelby set down her glass and took a long sip of the coffee their waitress had just delivered. What exactly was Jake proposing?

"What do you say? A little vacation would be good for both of us. Some time to be alone together, with nothing else in the way. Paul's supposed to be coming out for a visit, but I can get out of that. He'll understand."

She leaned back in her chair, clutching the edge of the table as if for support. "Jake," she said woodenly, as the full force of his words began to register, "I can't just drop everything and run off to the islands right now."

"I'm just talking about a couple of days," he interjected. "Till the storm blows over. That's all."

"I have responsibilities. Commitments." She gazed at him uncomprehendingly. "Can't you see that?"

"Of course I see that," he said defensively. "I also see the dark circles under your eyes, and since I'm largely responsible for putting them there, I thought the least I could do was . . ." His voice trailed off. Again he caught her hand in his own. "C'mon, Shelby," he urged gently. "The best rooms, the best restaurants, the tiniest bikinis you can find. Nothing's too good—or too sexy—for the woman I love."

*The woman I love.*

The words tugged at her soul. They'd come so easily to Jake, so effortlessly.

And that was just the problem—the problem she had tried all along to ignore. Jake's love was a temporary thing, sweet and ephemeral as the white rose he'd given her that night at the senator's. It cost him nothing to give, and in the long run it meant nothing.

"Jake," she whispered. "I can't."

"Whoa." He tightened his grip on her hand. "I think you missed something there. I just said 'I love you.' Isn't that the point where you say 'I love you, too,' or have I been watching the wrong movies?"

Shelby looked away, pulling free of his touch. She could not bear to see his face. "I . . . can't," she said again.

"Can't *what*, damn it? Can't go away with me? Or do you mean—" his words grew so soft she could barely make them out "—you can't say 'I love you'?

The hurt in his voice tore at her heart, but she couldn't bring herself to say the words he longed for. What was the point? What he wanted to hear today would mean nothing to him a year from now.

"Why?" she heard him asking. "Why can't you tell me what I know you're feeling, love?"

"Because," she struggled to control her quavering voice, "it has to *matter*. That's the whole point, don't you see? I can run off with you for a weekend, but what then?"

"Then we return to P-town and get back to work."

She kept on, knowing it was too late now to turn back. "And I can say 'I love you,' but what then? What then, Jake?"

He began to respond and then caught himself. Silence stretched between them. When he finally spoke, it was in a heavy voice, emotionless and flat. "I don't have that answer, Shelby," he told her levelly. "All I know is that I love you. That I never want to be without you. I'll do whatever it takes to keep you with me."

"Oh, Jake." Shelby's voice rose on a tide of bitter emotion. "What would you *do*?" She met his eyes reluctantly, afraid of the pain she would see in them; afraid of what he would see in hers. "Will you stay here in Provincetown? Are you going to live off your past glories, content to settle down in a small town, spend your afternoons telling tall tales at the local bar? Or do you want me to sail off into the sunset with you? Follow *your* dream?"

"Shelby. . ." he protested, but she knew her words had found their mark.

"Do you want me to give up my life, follow wherever you lead?" she continued relentlessly.

"Maybe so," Jake said softly, almost wistfully. "If you love me."

"And if I did all that, Jake," Shelby choked, "would you still love me? Without a life of my own, would you even *know* me?"

"Charity," Jake whispered, shaking his head sadly. "Charity Stetham."

It took Shelby only a moment to understand. "Exactly." She managed a melancholy smile. "You can't stay and become a 'gentleman farmer,'" and I won't run away to sea with you."

"But you love . . . the sea."

"Yes, Jake." She swallowed the hard lump in her throat. "I love . . . the sea. But sometimes love isn't enough."

Tears blurred her vision, and she blotted them away with her napkin. Why had he spoiled her sweet self-deception? Why had he spoken of love, and destroyed its promise at the same time? The truth she had tried to desperately to forget was out in the open. There could be no ignoring it now. There could be no going back.

She felt hollow, hopeless and defeated. And the worst part was she'd known it would all turn out this way. She'd let it happen.

"So have you folks decided?" The waitress had materialized at Shelby's side, bubbling with inexplicable cheerfulness.

"Yes," Shelby answered bitterly, shoving back her chair to depart. "I'm afraid we have."

NOW SHELBY WAS GRATEFUL for the rain. As she rushed from the tavern, sloshing indifferently through puddles, the weather seemed a perfect reflection of her mood.

She moved quickly, detouring through an alley to make it difficult for Jake to follow her. Not that she expected him to. He'd watched her leave the restaurant without uttering a word. At the door she'd allowed herself to look back at him for a brief moment, and he'd been sitting there at the table, arms crossed over his chest, watching her calmly. His face betrayed not the slightest hint of emotion.

Several minutes had passed before Shelby realized she was instinctively heading home. She stopped, umbrella poised over her head, and considered turning back toward Safeseas. But what was the point? She couldn't work right now; she couldn't even think straight. Nothing much seemed to matter except going home. It was all very simple: she would lock the door, pull down the shades and shut out the pain—for a while, at least.

But the quiet warmth of her apartment did nothing to unravel the tight knots in her chest. Crying seemed the logical thing to do, but she couldn't even seem to get that right. She sat immobilized on the sofa, Cipher's head in her lap, with a box of tissues placed strategically close at hand, and managed to produce only a couple of token hot tears.

What was wrong with her? If she couldn't even manage the appropriate response to a breakup, was it any wonder she couldn't get the relationship part down right?

She reached for the telephone on the end table. Maybe she needed someone to talk to. A friendly shoulder to cry—or in her case, not cry—on. Terry would know what to do. Shelby picked up the receiver, stared at it glumly and slowly dialed Terry's number.

She answered on the first ring.

Shelby could hear dishes clattering in the background. "You busy? It's me."

"That all depends on your definition. I've got two weeks' worth of dishes in the sink and two months' worth of laundry in the washer. Hey, are you okay? You sound kind of...I don't know, deflated."

"I suppose." She took a deep, quivery breath. "Jake and I...we, uh...sort of ended things."

"Oh, Shel—"

"Not that there was much to end." She tried to laugh, but the guttural sound from her throat was entirely unfamiliar.

"Where are you now? Home?" The tone of maternal authority in Terry's voice was remarkably comforting.

"Yeah. Me and Cipher."

"Stay put. I'll be there in five minutes. In the meantime, I want you to keep away from all sharp implements and Häagen-Dazs. Understand?"

True to her word, Terry was ascending the back staircase within minutes. Shelby held the door open, and Terry entered with a backward glance toward the driveway.

"You know he's here, don't you?" she whispered conspiratorially, slipping off her wet yellow rain slicker.

"Jake?" Shelby groaned. "Downstairs?"

Terry wrapped her arm around Shelby and led her to the couch. "He pulled in right as I walked up. Didn't say a word. I might as well have been invisible." She shook her head with a worldly, seen-it-all smile. "Men," she sighed, as though the wisdom of the ages were packaged in that one small syllable.

Shelby smiled in spite of herself. "You know, the truth is, I'm fine. I guess I just felt like some—"

Beneath their feet a door slammed loudly.

Shelby winced. "Some company. Actually I don't really feel much of anything. I've just lost the only man I've ever cared about, and all I feel is, well, numb."

"Denial," Terry pronounced wisely. "It's the most dangerous phase." She headed purposefully toward the kitchen and swung open the refrigerator door. "So. What'll it be? Ice cream? Popcorn? Brownies, perhaps?"

"Really, Terry. I'm not very hungry right now."

"Oh, my God." Terry shut the refrigerator door abruptly and rushed to join Shelby on the couch. "This is far more serious than I thought."

Another loud bang from the downstairs apartment set Shelby's teeth on edge. She looked at Terry's warm brown eyes and felt grateful for her friend's presence. "I suppose he's moving out to the *Questor*."

"It's probably just as well. You can both cool off a little."

"Oh, we were perfectly cool. That's the scary part. We both knew there was never any way to make it work. Finally one of us just had the nerve to say it out loud."

"And who *was* this trailblazer?" Terry asked disapprovingly.

"Okay, it was me. But he agreed, Terry. We both love our own lives too much to ever change."

"But you love each other even more," Terry offered gently.

Outside a car door slammed, and an engine roared to life.

Suddenly, inexplicably, Shelby felt hot tears streaming down her cheeks. "I don't," she choked, "understand—"

Teresa circled Shelby's heaving shoulders with her arm. "Phase two," she whispered, reaching for a tissue. "Acceptance."

## 11

"GREAT," SHELBY COMPLAINED tonelessly, "I can have a tuna sandwich or a nice healthy salad. There must be *something* chocolate in there."

She settled at last for graham crackers and peanut butter, half of which she fed to Cipher.

"Well," she said to her dog, "I've certainly handled everything beautifully, haven't I?" Cipher shifted position and kept his undivided attention focused on the remaining crackers. Crazy as it seemed, she'd begun to hope Jake would come home, that she would hear the bang of a door, the creak of the old four-poster, the scrape of the chair—the little sounds from the apartment below she'd grown so accustomed to.

And then?

And then she would pound on the floor and call out to him to come up those stairs, and they would forget all she had said; that she would put all her doubts out of her mind if only he would climb those stairs and take her in his arms.

But she had forbidden that, hadn't she? In her usual self-assured fashion she had been determined to let him know that no one, not even Jake Lawson, could sweep Shelby Haynes off her feet.

Shelby Haynes, Wonder Woman. See Shelby stand tall! See the great goddess of Stellwagen Bank hold off the ruthless Texas plunderer! She shook her head morosely. See Shelby Haynes trying to forget how hopelessly screwed up her life has become by eating everything in the house.

She rose lethargically from the couch, heading with a fatalistic shrug toward the kitchen.

Was he off on the *Questor* thinking of her? Working his way through a fifth of bourbon and trying to forget what had happened?

She hoped so.

She hoped not.

The refrigerator held no more promise than it had on the last trip. Well, she decided, when all else failed, make coffee. At least she would be alert in her misery.

With sudden clarity she recalled the first time they had met—Jake, dripping on the deck of the *Questor*, holding a mug of coffee.

It had all been impossible from the beginning: Jake and she were too much alike. A pair of willful, independent people, unaccustomed to compromise, never willing to give in. They were two ships that should have passed in the night and instead collided. Two prima donnas jostling for center stage.

That was part of what had made sex between them so magnificent. Love, however, was a different matter. She couldn't allow herself to love him.

Jake was an adventurer, a man who breezed into town, sweeping all before him with wondrous fairy tales of pirate treasure and doomed lovers. He was larger than life, dramatic, exciting; everything he touched was transformed.

And he had touched her. Touched her life; touched her heart and turned it to gold—then stolen it away, leaving only an aching emptiness behind.

Worse yet was the fact that she still faced long weeks, even months, with him near: in the room below, on the bridge of the *Questor*. Day in and day out, too near to begin to forget.

She wandered to the window and gazed out over the roofs of Provincetown to the sea beyond. The storm was moving offshore quickly now. Already the rain had stopped.

Somewhere out there under the blanket of night was the *Questor*, riding gentle swells at anchor. Jake would be getting ready to check the lines one last time and see that the mooring lights were on.

The lights.

The phrase stuck in her mind. She remembered last night—was it only last night?—in the Zodiac, warm in Jake's arms while a hundred yards away the *Questor* sat anchored, lights blazing in the dark.

There was something....

She shook her head in frustration. In the kitchen the coffee was done. She poured a cup and switched off the machine. The red brew light went out.

Almost unbidden, her finger reached for the light. It was warm to the touch.

Light and heat!

She set her cup down with shaking fingers.

That was it! Heat might not always make light, but where there was light, there was always heat.

And heat would show up on infrared film, especially the heat of a bright running light against a background of cold sea and night sky.

Shelby froze, recalling the infrared picture of Harold, his tail high in the air, and beyond him the indistinct shadow of a boat—the *Questor*.

*Not the* Questor *!*

Pausing only to grab a jacket, she raced for the door.

The streets seemed unnaturally empty, save for a few late bar patrons. Clouds left behind by the storm were migrating quickly out to sea, allowing intermittent peeks at the canopy of stars beyond.

Safeseas was locked and deserted—apparently even Tuan had to sleep sometime. She found the print in the dark-room where she had left it that morning and held it under the light.

Of course. How could she have been so blind?

The boat in the picture showed fairly strong heat regis-ters toward the stern, where the engines gave off heat. But where the lights should have shown up as brilliant points, there was nothing.

This boat, whatever it was, had been running without lights—and that was not only unsafe, it was illegal. Clearly its crew had not wished to be seen. And at that distance, a muffled engine would not have been heard above the sounds of the sea.

Using a magnifying glass, Shelby traced the indistinct outline of the boat with a fine point marker. Immediately it became clear that this streamlined, low-slung craft was not the somewhat ungainly former research vessel that Jake had renamed *Questor*. This was the silhouette of a yacht, the plaything of a rich man.

Or of a corporation.

But what was the mystery boat doing out there, sneak-ing around in the dark? What was its connection, if any, to the mishaps aboard the *Questor*?

It could well have been responsible for cutting the *Ques-tor* adrift, but why would it return to the scene of the crime the following night? Certainly the fire and the equipment troubles—not to mention the sabotaging of her air tanks—all had to have been done by one of Jake's crew.

Nevertheless, this particular yacht had not been out for a pleasure cruise. Of that she was certain.

Shelby took a deep steadying breath and walked down the hall to the tiny closet of a room where the radio was kept. She switched on the power, but when she lifted the mike to her mouth, she found she could not speak.

She had to call him; it was that simple. But when he heard her voice, he would leap to conclusions, one way or the other. If she heard coldness in his voice, it would be unbearable. If she heard elation, it would kill her.

This was business, she told herself. Just basic courtesy, really. Not to tell Jake what she had discovered would be irresponsible.

Besides, like it or not, she had become part of this fight.

Steeling herself, she depressed the "send" key.

"Safeseas One, calling *Questor*."

JAKE SAT IN A FOLDING CHAIR on the foredeck of the *Questor*, gazing back toward Provincetown's faint, far-off lights. He had sent J.B. ashore for the night, fully intending to drown his sorrows in alcohol, but the glass of Scotch sat barely touched on the deck beside him. Paul Richardson and Tim Murphy were coming out to the site the next day, and it wouldn't look too good for him to be nursing a hangover. Besides, this was not a pain he could ease with booze.

Time and again he replayed the argument in his head, trying to disprove all that Shelby had said... trying to convict her of being irrational and stubborn. But each time he came up against the same truth: he had no answers.

He had just assumed that when he confessed his love for her, she would see that they had to be together, that day-to-day realities would shrivel to insignificance beside that transcendent fact.

And yet...

Would he be content to stay here in Provincetown? Yes, for a while perhaps.

He snorted derisively at his own dishonesty. *Come on, Jake,* he chided himself, *tell the truth. She's got your num-*

*ber. Shelby's right. You'll never be satisfied here, resting on your laurels. Every day you'd wake up and look out at the ocean and wish you were on it—challenging it, uncovering its secrets.*

Already he had several new projects in mind—plans that would take him far from here once the *Evangeline* was his.

But if Shelby wasn't with him, his heart could never be in it. Because his heart would always belong to her. He took a swig of his whiskey, but the taste was bitter in his mouth, and he tossed the remaining liquid overboard.

Shelby, he thought with fond sadness, would probably yell at him for that—intoxicating the sea life or some such thing. He wondered how he would ever bear having her near, standing here on this deck, day after day, never to touch her, never to—

From the bridge he heard the muffled crackling of the radio.

"Probably Janine calling to make sure I haven't done myself in," he muttered dryly, but he climbed to his feet and ambled toward the bridge.

"Safeseas One, calling *Questor*, come in."

It was not Janine.

It didn't make any sense, Shelby calling him here. There was nothing left for either of them to say.

Still, the mere sound of her voice made all things seem possible. . . .

"Jake, this is Shelby. Come in, please."

Taking a deep breath, he keyed the "send" button.

"Shelby? What's up?" He tried to sound nonchalant, but his voice carried the weight of his heart.

"Jake, I have to talk to you." The voice came, tinny and distorted, but hers. "It's about the *Questor*, and the salvage, but I need to see you privately to explain. Jake, I'm afraid—" she hesitated and he heard the worry in her tone. "I don't want to explain over the air."

"Shelby, are you in some kind of trouble?"

"No, no. I'm fine. But . . . can you meet me? Soon? I . . . have a hunch."

"You don't play hunches."

"All right. Call it a theory."

Jake considered for a moment. Clearly it was important. But just as clearly it was not about them. In any case, what choice did he have?

"I'm the only one on board and the launch is ashore, so I'll have to bring the *Questor* in. Can you meet me at the wharf in half an hour?"

"I'll be waiting in my car."

"Are you sure you're all right?" he pressed.

"Jake, I'm fine," she said softly, adding, as though an afterthought, "and please, be careful. It's dark out there."

The radio fell silent, and Jake heard his heart pounding in the sudden quiet.

TWENTY-FIVE MINUTES LATER Jake was striding purposefully toward her car, which she'd run home from Safeseas to retrieve. She sat now in the nearly empty wharf parking lot, idling the engine so she wouldn't have to face restarting it.

Jake pulled open the door and settled his big frame next to her on the seat, filling the compartment with a compellingly male scent that was part ocean, part salt air and part something indefinably his own. His very nearness seemed a kind of seduction, and she clung to the battered green steering wheel as though to stabilize herself. She had to start learning not to react to him this way. *Had* to, or there was no hope of freeing herself from his spell.

"Good," he said. "You're all right. I was worried." It was a statement of fact, without emotional timbre. "What did you want to tell me?"

"I hope this isn't a wild-goose chase—" Shelby began.

"I've had my share. Don't worry." He was not smiling. Even in the dark she could see that.

"Well, it's a long story. To begin with, that infrared film we had with us the other night picked up the outline of another boat out there with us. A big one."

"Impossible. We would have seen it."

"We *were* otherwise occupied for a while," she said, pressing past the emotion in her voice. "And its running lights were off."

"I see."

"Anyway, it looked familiar. I'm pretty sure it's a yacht owned by a big company called CCI that has its headquarters here on the Cape. You met their chairman at the senator's the other night." Shelby thought she saw a faint grimace twist his lips. "I think they keep their boat docked down south in Eastham."

"And you figure they're tied into our problems on the *Questor*?"

"What do you think?" Shelby replied anxiously.

"I think you've figured it just right. And something else is beginning to occur to me." He fell silent in thought, not encouraging any further queries.

After a long moment Jake turned to her. "Where did you say that yacht was docked?"

"Eastham. It's another town south of here. Twenty minutes by car, give or take."

"If you saw it again, could you be reasonably sure it was the boat in the photo?" he asked.

"Better than that. I brought the picture."

Jake nodded thoughtfully. "Then how would you like to take a little road trip down to this Eastham place?"

THEIR VISIT to the Eastham marina amply confirmed Shelby's suspicions. There could be no doubt that the Cape Cod Industries boat was the vessel in the picture. Jake grimly concurred with her opinion.

It was nearly midnight when they returned to the outskirts of Provincetown. Fatigue—emotional and physical—had finally begun to take its toll on Shelby, and Jake had insisted on driving the Dodge on the trip back. She fought the desire to curl up in the soft, inviting harbor of his arm and instead huddled uncomfortably against the unforgiving sharp angles of the passenger door.

She awoke to the feel of Jake's fingertips caressing her cheek.

"We're back," he said curtly, drawing away.

She couldn't mistake his all-business tone. "So now what?" she asked drowsily.

"Now I confront the crew and weed out the traitor. He is more than likely on CCI's payroll."

"But why? Why would a company like that go to all this trouble just to stop you from digging?"

"That remains to be seen," he said gravely. "But I have some suspicions that may bear fruit." His gaze traveled her body with the palpable effect of touch. "You look tired."

"You don't look so hot yourself." And in fact, he didn't. He looked drawn and anxious in his wrinkled work shirt and faded jeans.

"I want to thank you for coming to me with this information," Jake told her with the first real smile she'd seen since he'd climbed into the car. "I know how difficult it must have been."

"Actually," she answered thoughtfully, "it wasn't difficult at all. Not really. I thought I could help, and that's all that seemed to matter... at the time." She traced a finger along her dusty dashboard absentmindedly. "Was it difficult for you? Coming to see me, I mean?"

"Not at all. I was scared to death you might have been in some kind of trouble. As a matter of fact—" he nodded toward the floorboard "—I jumped ashore so fast I forgot to put on any shoes."

They laughed quietly, dissipating some of the tension that had frosted the atmosphere in the car.

"Shelby?" Jake murmured. "I..." He stopped, as though unsure of how, or whether, to proceed. When he began again, his voice had recovered some of its old self-assurance. "I realize there are a lot of unresolved problems between us—"

Shelby started to speak, to tell him that there were no problems between them—that there must be *nothing* between them—but their gazes tangled, and she lost the careful words. "Yes," she answered finally, "there are still problems between us."

"The thing is, whatever our difficulties, I think I need your help. I'm afraid you're the only one I can fully trust."

Her eyes burned with unbidden tears at the naked simplicity of his admission. "Are you going to tell me what this is all about?" she managed.

"I'll tell you what it's not about. It's not about the *Evangeline*. CCI is not the sort of outfit that would go in for buried treasure. They don't have the imagination for it."

"But if they're trying to stop you from the hunt, then—" She stopped in confusion. "That makes no sense."

"Maybe it's not the treasure they're worried about." His lips were compressed in a grim line. "Maybe there's something else they don't want us to find."

"But what would CCI want to hide in the ocean?"

"Cape Cod Industries Incorporated," Jake recited. "Leaders in plastics, precision machine tools, telecommunications—" his voice dropped to a sad whisper "—and if you believe their advertising . . . chemical research."

Shelby felt a cold hand clutch at her heart. "Tim Murphy—"

"Is coming to the *Questor* for lunch today along with Paul Richardson," Jake finished. "Not much time to spin our web."

"Not much time," she agreed, staring off in concentration. "We can get what we need at Safeseas."

WITHIN AN HOUR they were back aboard the *Questor* and pulling away from the dock. While Jake guided the boat expertly around the marker buoys, Shelby switched on a bright light over the chart table behind him.

She spread out the navigational chart of the general search area and located the mark indicating the precise mooring of the *Questor* on the night of the stakeout. Next she laid out the photograph showing the CCI yacht.

"Okay," she muttered, her brow lined in concentration, "the *Questor*'s there." She placed the sharp tip of a compass on the location. "And we were in the Zodiac about there to start with, but with the sea anchor and a slow current . . . let's say we were right about there. So . . . the CCI boat had to be downwind from us, or we'd have heard the engines even at low idle. Hmm."

She rummaged across the table and found a pocket calculator. "You know, you should be doing this," she complained. "It's been years since I had to do any mathematical heavy lifting."

Jake smiled. "Someone has to drive."

Ahead to the east the sun had risen on a day of crystal clarity.

"Okay," Shelby continued her self-directed conversation. "I think I've got his location, roughly. Thank goodness for calculators. Logarithms give me hives."

Searching through a map case she had borrowed from Safeseas, she located a large topographical map of the ocean floor. She laid it out on the table and with a long ruler drew fine pencil lines from the side and bottom until they intersected.

"Ah!" She looked up, her eyes glowing. "Got him!"

Since they were safely clear of the harbor and rounding Race Point, Jake set the wheel and joined Shelby.

"Here." She pointed to the chart. "He was directly over this fissure here." Jake peered over her shoulder at what looked like a steep valley in the undulating floor of the ocean. "Its far deeper than the surrounding area. Even if a diver were in the water around there, he probably wouldn't notice the fissure unless he was right on top of it, or looking for it. It could be the result of seismic activity, or there could be an underwater spring."

"An underwater spring?" Jake echoed incredulously.

"Sure. The same sort of thing that would give you a pond or a lake on land. The water table around here is strange. That's why we have 365 ponds and lakes on the Cape."

"So there might actually be water flowing up out of that trench."

"Could be." Shelby shrugged. "Or it could be just a normal fissure."

"Interesting," Jake commented thoughtfully. "I think that might prove to be a useful notion."

Within a matter of minutes they had reached the area. Shelby listened pensively as Jake radioed the *Questor*'s new position to a puzzled Greg at the crew hotel. He deliberately gave Greg no explanation for the change in location or for his subsequent order.

"I want you and the rest of the crew to wait ashore till Senator Richardson and...and his guest arrive. They're due to be at the wharf at 11:00 a.m."

"Uh, sure, Captain." The puzzlement in Greg's voice was clear even through the radio's distortion. "But we could come on out and send one person back—"

"No," Jake snapped, "Just do as I said." He replaced the radio transmitter softly.

Shelby could see the pain in his eyes. He wasn't a man accustomed to mistrust. Yet he had to assume that one of the five crew members was a saboteur—a traitor responsible for all the mishaps that had plagued his hunt. And Shelby knew what Jake did not: that the same saboteur might have nearly caused her death.

"They'll think I've gone nuts," Jake remarked ruefully.

"They trust you."

"Four of them do." He sighed. "The other...well, the other might smell a rat, but whoever he is, he has to show up. Or she," he added as an afterthought.

"Janine?" Shelby scoffed. "No way. It isn't her."

"Then who?" Jake demanded. "Greg? It he's the one, then Janine's probably in it with him. Marcus? Hell, he's an old pro with a family to think of. Thomas, J.B.?" Jake hesitated, as a shadow of memory passed over his face. "J.B.'s a kid," he said, but his voice betrayed uncertainty.

Shelby stepped toward him and took his hand. "I know this must be awful for you, having to suspect people you want to trust."

Tension tightened the cords in his neck. "I feel...well, I just don't like it." He shook his head. "I don't like having to trick them this way. I feel like I'm betraying them somehow."

"Jake, don't. Listen to me. The ones who are innocent may have some hurt feelings at first, but when they've had a chance to think it over, they'll know you did what you had to do."

At least she hoped they'd understand, she mused silently. The plan she and Jake had been working out was risky—a bluff at best. Or, as Jake had put it, "too cute by half." But with no sleep and little time, it was all they could think of—and their only real hope.

"Yes, maybe you're right." Jake shook himself out of his dark reverie. "Anyway, we have work to do. One of us has to check the equipment, and the other has to whip up something to serve our guests."

Shelby held up a hand. "I'll get right on that equipment check."

THE SUN ROSE HIGH, burning the mist from the sea and warming the deck of the *Questor*. Heat conspired with a lack of sleep to turn Shelby's limbs to jelly and her eyelids to lead. After she'd finished checking and rechecking everything, she sank into a deck chair, determined to rest her eyes for just a moment or two. In the galley she could hear Jake busily banging pans and whistling as though he hadn't a care in the world.

He'd had his moment of doubt, she realized, but now he knew what he had to do and was determined to get on with it. It must be nice to be able to set aside doubt so easily.

Her eyes fluttered open, then closed more tightly.

"I'm awake. I'm awake." She jerked her head up and opened her eyes.

"Sure you are." Jake laughed. "And you've been awake for the past three hours. You've just been very, very quiet. Here, sleeping beauty."

Shelby took the glass of iced coffee from his hand. "Oh, I'm sorry." She swept her hair back, combing it with her fingers. "Why didn't you wake me up?"

"Wasn't any point. Besides, it wouldn't hurt if at least one of us was alert."

"What time is it?"

"Twenty after eleven. Greg just radioed to say they're on their way out with Paul."

"And Murphy?"

Jake nodded with grim satisfaction. "And Murphy."

Shelby swallowed half the contents of the glass and rose to her feet. Together they made their way toward the stern where Jake had set up a long table surrounded by folding chairs. Shelby whistled appreciatively. "Tablecloth and everything."

"Well, it's not exactly crystal and sterling silver, but we *are* having a member of the Senate to lunch."

"We're also having a snake. Or two."

Jake looked up and pointed casually toward the land. "There they are."

The heavily laden launch was making its way across a sea of bright glass. A slight offshore breeze carried the sound of the outboard engine as it churned up a plume of spray.

"Oh, Jake, do you really think this will work?"

"It has to," Jake answered softly, "because I want the SOB."

Suddenly Shelby remembered the feeling of losing consciousness in the icy black water as her tanks failed; remembered the whales washed up dead on the beach . . . so many of them. Jake was right. It had to work. Because the slaughter had to stop, and someone had to pay.

"Not as much as I want him."

## 12

THE ZODIAC PULLED ALONGSIDE, and Marcus jumped aboard the *Questor* to help Senator Richardson and Tim Murphy on deck. Shelby searched the faces of the crew. Janine and Greg seemed guarded and vaguely worried. J.B. looked slightly puzzled, as though he'd just heard something he didn't quite believe. Marcus appeared annoyed—probably at having to be polite to two strangers. Thomas headed off immediately to check his engines, without a word to anyone.

Richardson met Jake with a politician's hearty handshake. "So where's the gold?" he joked loudly.

Jake played along, smiling tightly. "It's around here somewhere," he said, gesturing toward the water. He turned to Tim Murphy. "Mr. Murphy, welcome aboard."

The slightly built executive managed a sour smile. "Thanks for having me, Captain Lawson. Although, since I opposed your expedition here, I feel a bit like I'm visiting an enemy camp."

It was intended as a joke, but Shelby could see the dangerous light in Jake's eyes as he responded. "Yes. I'll bet you do."

She stepped forward quickly. "Uh, Jake, why don't you show these gentlemen around? I'm sure—"

Murphy interrupted her. "Yes, I'd like to see how it's done. Are we over the treasure site right now?"

"We haven't narrowed it down that precisely yet," Jake explained. "We'd been concentrating over to the east about a quarter of a mile, where Shelby found the snuffbox, but I've decided to try over here for a while."

Greg was scanning the horizon, as if trying to get his bearings by points on land. "This is over by the spot where we lost the magnetometer," he said, "if I'm not too far off in my—"

"Yes," Jake cut in. "Right where we lost the mag." He took a deep breath and forced the grimness out of his voice. "I was looking over the charts again, and I saw some interesting topographical features here. There's a trench right under us."

Shelby, her eyes glued on Murphy's face, caught his barely controlled spasm at the word "trench."

"Ms Haynes here suggested it might be an underwater spring. Anyway, it occurred to me that this trench might have served as a sort of catchall for the treasure. Ocean current and natural silting might have deposited at least some artifacts there."

Shelby watched Greg nodding in agreement. No doubt the superficially plausible argument explained for him Jake's somewhat strange behavior. But when she turned to look at the rest of the crew, she found Janine staring at her with disconcerting intensity, as though searching for answers in Shelby's face.

"Interesting," Murphy commented coldly.

"Hell, it must be great," Richardson said, trying to ease the apparent hostility between Jake and the industrialist. "Out here, breathing the fresh salt air every day, sunshine and blue sky and the quest for sunken treasure. While *I* have to breathe the majority leader's cigar smoke in some windowless committee room and talk about funding for the department of widgets, weirdos and waste in Washington."

The joke brought smiles all around. Marcus actually laughed out loud.

Nervous laughter, Shelby wondered, or was she just getting paranoid?

"Like that, my friend?" Richardson asked Marcus, shaking his hand. "I have to confess it's from my last campaign stump speech. You are a registered voter, I hope?"

"All right, Paul, no campaigning at sea," Jake chided, keeping the mood light. "Come on and I'll show you both around before we sit down to lunch." He led Richardson and Murphy toward the bridge.

Shelby began to follow, but Janine took her arm and drew her away from the others.

"All right, Shelby. I know it's none of my business what goes on between you two, but the captain looks terrible."

"What do you mean?" Shelby asked.

"I mean, he seems so edgy, so strange. And for that matter, so do you. Have you had a fight?"

"A fight?" she echoed. How strange to be reminded here, now. Was that what had Janine worried, or was this merely a clever cover for her real concern? "I don't really think—"

"I know, it's none of my business." Janine sighed. "It's just that, well, I'd gotten used to seeing him happy. It's so sad to see him like this."

Shelby was at a loss for words, a silence Janine seemed to interpret as a reproach.

"All right, I'll stay out of it. I just want to say one thing— if you let him go, you're a lot dumber than I give you credit for." She stalked away, almost angrily, before Shelby could react.

Now what was that all about? Shelby wondered. Or was it about anything? Suspicion was like a drug: it distorted everything. The day before she would have seen the conversation as a touching expression of concern. Now it seemed more like a subtle inquisition.

She heard men's voices and looked up to see Jake returning with their two guests.

"...so in other words," Richardson was saying, "you can't just go down and look for something shiny because it's going to be covered with corrosion and barnacles."

"Well, the silver will have actually turned black, and of course any iron will have rusted thoroughly. Gold holds up the best, of course, but as heavy as it is, it'll often settle and become completely covered by shifting sand or marine plant life. In fact, if you don't know just what to look for, you could dive right on top of a sunken ship and never know it."

Tim Murphy seemed uninvolved in the discussion, his icy blue eyes darting about impatiently as he was led to the table.

Shelby exchanged an anxious look with Jake and crossed her fingers behind her back. The crew members, unusually subdued, took their places while Jake ducked into the galley. He returned with a steaming pot, which he set in the middle of the table.

"That smells great. This fresh air has given me a tremendous appetite," Richardson said. "What is it?"

"Jambalaya," Jake announced as he began to ladle out the thick stew onto their plates. "Cajun, and very spicy."

"Oh, so the galley war continues," J.B. said somewhat unhappily. "I'm going to have to get a recipe book."

"Mmm. Great," Richardson commented. "Excellent. Did Ms Haynes produce this gastronomic masterpiece?"

"No." Shelby shook her head. "Captain Lawson is the chef."

"Oh, well, then." The senator shrugged. "Then it's passable. Say, did Jake here ever tell you about the time in the army when we were out on a three-day hike and he tried to make Cherries Jubilee using some wild gooseberries we picked? He was going to show all of us slobs how to live well, even in the middle of the forest. Had it going, too, till he tried to use cough syrup to flambé it. For about a month everyone called him Jubilee Jake." Richardson laughed, and Jake, looking slightly embarrassed, joined in.

"Excuse me, Captain Lawson," Tim Murphy said, "this is really very good, but rather spicy. Do you have something to drink?"

Shelby felt her heart tighten in apprehension. "I'll get some water," she heard herself respond automatically.

"I'd offer you some wine, Mr. Murphy," Jake explained, watching Shelby rise. "But we don't indulge during the day. Alcohol and scuba diving go together as poorly as alcohol and driving."

"Water's fine," Murphy said.

"However," Jake continued as Shelby returned with a full pitcher, "we do have something of a treat—a curiosity, if you will."

Beginning with Jake, Shelby began filling all the glasses on the table.

"You remember," Jake explained, "I mentioned we thought the trench beneath us might have been formed by an underwater freshwater spring? Well, we dropped a hose over this morning, just to check out our theory, and sure enough—" he put the glass to his lips and made a satisfied sound "—pure spring water from beneath the sea."

"Wow," J.B. commented, holding up his glass to examine it.

Shelby filled Murphy's glass last.

Jake lifted his tumbler into the air. "As discoverer of this spring and captain of the *Questor*, I hereby dub this Shelby's Spring in honor of Ms Haynes, and raise my glass in toast."

As though in slow motion, Shelby watched as Richardson raised his glass, smiling over at her; as J.B. and Marcus followed; as Greg sniffed his suspiciously and Janine nudged him and then raised her own.

Everyone joined in the toast—except one.

Tim Murphy sat staring awkwardly down at the table, trying to make himself invisible.

But Shelby was confused. All five crew members had drunk the water. One should have refused!

"It's not polite to refuse to join in a toast, Mr. Murphy," Jake said, his voice dangerously silky.

"I'm not thirsty."

"Oh? A moment ago you were."

"Well, I'm not now," Murphy snapped.

"Still, common courtesy. . ." Jake let it hang.

"I said I'm not thirsty, damn it!"

By now all eyes were on Murphy. Richardson nodded slightly to himself, as though something he had suspected was at last becoming clear.

"And I say you will not show such rudeness on my boat!" Jake snapped. "Drink it." He rose from his seat.

Murphy's mouth worked as the color rose in his cheeks. He reached for the glass, but his hand stopped in midair. Jake stood over him threateningly as the crew looked on in wide-eyed amazement.

Finally Jake seemed to lose patience. Grabbing the still half-full pitcher, he pressed it to Murphy's lips.

"Drink it, you bastard. Or wear it!"

With those words he emptied the pitcher on Murphy's head. The effect was immediate and startling.

Murphy screamed, leaping to his feet and yanking at the tablecloth to dry himself. "Get it off me! Get it off!" Dishes went flying as he pulled at the tablecloth, and the other diners jumped back to avoid the ensuing mess.

"Jeez, it's like Dorothy and the Wicked Witch of the West," J.B. said in astonishment as Murphy tore frantically at his shirt.

But Jake had clearly had enough. He grabbed Murphy urgently by the shoulders and pinned him against the railing.

"Something wrong with the water from that trench, Mr. Murphy?"

"Just get it off me!"

Jake laughed harshly. "Where did you get that water, Shelby?"

Shelby edged closer with grim satisfaction. "Right out of the tap."

Murphy stopped struggling. He was silent for a long moment, and when he looked up, his face was again composed. He began rebuttoning his shirt.

"Very nicely done, Captain Lawson," he said coolly. "Very clever. You of course knew I would never touch anything that came out of that trench. Just out of curiosity, is there a spring there or—"

Jake shook his head. "Just a big hole in the ground, as far as we know."

"Yes. A very convenient hole in the ground. What a pity we couldn't keep you away from it, even with the unwitting help of Ms Haynes." He managed a half smile. "Now I'd like to return to shore. I have a meeting in an hour, and I would like to change my clothes."

"You'll get a change of clothing—to a striped suit. And the only meeting you're going to have is with the police," Shelby said.

To Shelby's amazement, Murphy laughed.

"The police? What on earth for? For a violation of environmental regulations?"

"For dumping hazardous chemicals in the ocean!" Shelby exploded. "For killing more than a dozen whales in the past few months!"

"Ah, whale murder," Murphy mocked. "There's a crime for you." He shrugged. "Listen, Ms Haynes. I'll tell you what happens next. First, an investigation is launched by the state, and in a year, or two or three, they conclude there has been illegal dumping here. Then they threaten to file charges against CCI. CCI in turn hires the best law firm in Boston and tells the state that we intend to fight the allegations tooth and nail.

"Then the state calculates how many millions of dollars it would take to prosecute a case that could drag on in the courts for ten years, and they come to us with an offer—if CCI will pay for the cleanup and promise to be good, they will drop all charges. We will agree. End of story. Now—" he grinned savagely "—I'd like to go, unless you plan to hold me hostage."

Shelby shot a desperate glance at Jake. Beside him Richardson raised his eyebrows in a grim confirmation of Murphy's scenario.

"Maybe killing helpless, beautiful animals isn't enough to put you away, Murphy," Shelby said, her voice brittle in the sudden silence, "but attempted murder of a human being is."

Murphy's mask of self-assurance fell away.

"That's right—attempted murder," Shelby repeated more forcefully. "Because you're not the only snake on board here. You have a friend—or should I say coconspirator?"

She turned her gaze on the crew and almost lost her nerve. The looks of shock and betrayal cut to her heart. "Someone here had to slice the magnetometer cable just as we traversed this area. Someone had to set the fire in the chart room. Someone saw to it the *Questor* was cut adrift. And someone tried to kill me by poisoning my air tanks."

"What the hell—" Jake began, but his stunned query was cut short by Tim Murphy's angry explosion.

"You dumb son of a bitch! I never told you to kill anyone!"

"Shut up, you fool!" Marcus spat. "She's got no proof. She left the tanks. They're a mile down."

Shelby turned to face the older man. "That's right, Marcus," she agreed quietly. "But I had blood tests done right afterward, and they showed carbon monoxide. What did you do, Marcus, run a line from the engine exhaust?"

"I had nothing to do with that!" Murphy backed away. "He did that on his own!"

"You said stop them, Murphy. Stop them and it would be worth a hundred Gs. And it would have been perfect. If anything had happened to her, cops would have been running all over the place, I guarantee you. It would have looked as if Lawson did it to get her out of the way of the salvage. The papers would have gotten ahold of it, and it would have put an end to the whole thing."

"But murder?" Murphy growled. "No. It wasn't worth that."

"Why, Marcus?" J.B. broke in. "You would have made ten times that when we found the treasure."

Marcus laughed loudly. "Treasure? Don't make me laugh. I can't spend what I don't have."

Jake stepped forward and looked steadily into the man's face until Marcus turned away in confusion.

"You must have known what was in that trench," Jake pointed out. "Why did you drink the water?"

Marcus snorted in derision. "Because, unlike this jumped-up little weasel—" he pointed at Murphy "—I'm a poker player. And I know a bluff when I see one."

Jake moved as though to remove Marcus's smug grin in the most direct way possible, but Shelby put her hand on his shoulder, restraining him.

"Not always," she said softly. "You see, there never were any blood tests. And you're right—without the tanks, we had no evidence. Except, of course, for the confession you just gave us." She favored him with a coldly triumphant smile. "A confession heard by six willing witnesses, including a United States senator."

The reference seemed to rouse Paul Richardson. "Young man," he said to J.B., "if you'll show me how to operate the radio, I'll call the Coast Guard to come out and pick these two up. You could probably make the call yourself, Jake, but I think they might get here a little faster if I talk to them."

"Thanks, Paul." Jake turned to Greg and Janine. "Would you two check my tanks and break out the video camera, please?"

Shelby knew Jake always checked his own tanks. He was, she realized, attempting in a very real way to reassert his faith in the crew.

"Would you please check my tanks, as well, Greg?" she asked.

Jake spun to face her. "Oh, no, you don't. I'm not about to allow you to go down there with me."

"You're not going to *allow*?"

"That's right." Jake put his fists on his hips, staring hard at her. "It could be dangerous down there. This is my problem."

"Baloney!" Shelby shot back vehemently. "Excuse me. Baloney, Captain! This is actually my problem now, and if anyone should stay out of it, it's you."

"Me stay out of it!" he exploded.

"Yes, this is a job for—"

"Stop it!" Janine's exasperated shriek froze them both. "Listen, you two, if you ask me, the only thing that's clear here is that the problem belongs to both of you."

Shelby and Jake quickly turned to her, then slowly turned back toward each other.

"I don't remember asking her, do you?" Shelby asked calmly.

"No," Jake agreed. "But it could be she's right."

"We'll need to use 'dry' suits," Shelby remarked. "That way we'll be completely covered."

"That's safe enough, then." Jake nodded. "Say, you're more experienced than I am at underwater filming. Would you—"

Shelby smiled. "I'd be glad to."

DESPITE THE BRILLIANT SUN and the vacant blue sky, Shelby felt a shiver overtake her as she sat poised on the side of the boat, completely encased in her "dry" suit. She turned and gave Jake the thumbs-up sign, and with a nod he rolled backward into the sea. Holding tight to her camera with one hand and keeping her fiberglass helmet steady with the other, Shelby shifted her weight back and fell with a depth-charge splash into water carbonated by the bubbles from Jake's regulator.

"Be sure to write," she heard someone yell as the water closed over her head. Twisting around, she saw Jake several feet below, transiting a shaft of light. She gave a few powerful kicks and caught up with him, then settled into his steady pace, keeping just behind him and to one side.

They descended slowly, as in a dream of falling, drawn against their natural buoyancy by the heavy weight belts around their waists. Turning to look back, Shelby could see the dark hull of the *Questor*, a shadow on a sheet of glass, already part of another world. The light was becoming dimmer, robbing the fish that passed by of all color. She decided to switch on the pair of brilliant lights attached to the camera. Caught in the beam, a handsome bluefish turned to gape. The sandy, sloping bottom was only a dozen feet below them now, and ahead the sudden drop of the trench. Shelby saw Jake turn and motion her to follow him, staying at what, on dry land, would have been rooftop level.

After several hundred yards she noticed Jake had snapped on his own smaller, hand-held torch and was playing it ahead in slow arcs. His pace had slowed, and suddenly he stopped, motioning for her to do likewise. His rubber-encased hand gripped her arm, while he aimed his light steadily ahead.

There, on the sloping side of the deep trough, was a barrel, rusted brown, caught in the yellow beam of the flashlight. Instinctively Shelby switched on her camera as Jake led them downward at a shallow angle. As they descended, a surreal tableau unfolded: first a few, then dozens, and finally close to a hundred barrels, lying helter-skelter like the headstones of some bizarre graveyard. They kept above the barrels, traversing the chasm until they were able to see the full extent of the dump. Some of the barrels were pock-marked with barnacles, some others still had most of their danger-orange paint. And some, Shelby saw in the camera's viewfinder, still bore the logo of CCI.

Shelby kept her camera rolling even as Jake signaled her to return with him to the surface. Slowly the burying ground dwindled below, while her rage expanded to engulf her. It was as bad as their worst suspicions. Cape Cod Industries had been dumping illegally in her ocean! In poor Harold's ocean! Lord only knows what was in those barrels—what was leaking out of those barrels, by the look of them.

There could no longer be any doubt. This was the cause of the mysterious illness that was killing the whales on Stellwagen Bank. And this was the reason that CCI would go to any length to keep Jake from digging for the *Evangeline*. They must have realized he was bound to uncover their dirty secret eventually. She and Jake would be safe from the toxic effects, breathing bottled air and insulated by their suits, but the animals who lived out here had no such protection. This was where they lived and fed and brought up their young. And it was the young who had been especially vulnerable.

As soon as they broke the surface, Shelby tore off her helmet and looked for Jake. He was only a few feet away, looking gray with a depth of anger she had never witnessed in him before.

"There's so much!" she cried.

"Bastards," he cursed. "I hope the Coast Guard gets here fast, before I do something I'll regret to those two."

"But now what? What about the whales and the rest of the marine life? We have to . . . we have to do something."

"We will," Jake assured her. "We will, I promise you that."

## 13

SHELBY PAUSED with her hand on the cold brass doorknob. This was very nearly the last place on earth she wanted to be, but it was also the only place in Boston where she had not yet asked for help.

After a day and a half of bouncing from one state office to another, she saw that a definite pattern was beginning to emerge: everyone had some airtight excuse for why it would take well into the twenty-first century before Stellwagen Bank could be cleaned up. Tests, departmental oversight, budget crunches . . . the reasons varied, but the answer was invariably the same: no way.

Well, they always say it's not what you know, but who you know, she reflected, and she only knew one person in this bureaucratic maze.

She opened the door.

"May I help you, Miss?" a young, bespectacled secretary asked distractedly, focusing all her attention on the humming word processor in front of her.

Shelby glanced uncomfortably around the room. A narrow hallway to her left appeared to lead to several private offices, but the high-ceilinged reception area was empty, save for the secretary and her.

"I don't actually have an appointment, but I need to see someone about the toxic dumping in Stellwagen Bank."

The secretary kept her eyes glued to the glowing screen. "And you are?"

"Shelby Haynes, from the Safeseas Institute in Province-town. I'm director of cetacean research."

This time the secretary did look up. "What research?" she asked incredulously.

Shelby smiled. "Whales."

"You ought to see her with crayfish," came a voice that seemed at once strange and familiar.

She turned, extending her hand automatically, hoping he would not feel the need to embrace.

"Hello, Steve," she said, keeping her voice carefully neutral. Was this really him? Was this really the man she'd lost so many nights' sleep over?

"It's been a long time, Shel." Steve hugged her stiffly. "You look great." He stood back to look her over.

"You, too," she lied unconvincingly. He seemed different, shorter than she remembered—a perception perhaps due to the conspicuous increase in his girth. He had the same look basically: rumpled, vaguely preppy clothes; the dark-rimmed glasses propped low on his patrician nose. But his studied, self-conscious intensity seemed silly now rather than intimidating. In fact, the most noticeable change in Steve was just how very ordinary he'd become.

Or was it she who had changed?

"Come on," Steve said, gesturing toward the hall. "We can chat more comfortably in my office. Hold all my calls, Marsha."

Shelby caught the secretary's bewildered stare as Steve shepherded his former wife toward his private office, an uncluttered room with a window overlooking an alley.

She took the chair in front of his desk and smiled at the brown paper lunch bag by his phone.

"Obviously I'm interrupting your lunch," she said, nodding at the bag and a steaming cup of coffee. "I'm awfully sorry."

"No problem." He patted his stomach. "I could use a little diet. Besides—" he smiled genuinely "—I'd much rather reminisce with my favorite . . ."

"Ex-wife?" Shelby supplied. "Actually I'm not here to trade stories, Steve. It's about the dumping at Stellwagen."

"Ah." Steve leaned back in his leather chair, arms behind his head in a pose Shelby found uncharacteristically casual. "I should have known it would be business with you. But it is a damned shame about that mess. You realize we have a team out there right now to assess the situation? From what I'm hearing, things are under control. The barrels are more or less intact, and it sounds like CCI's going to be cooperative."

"Cooperative?" Shelby exclaimed, louder than she'd intended. "Tim Murphy's admitted there's something a lot like dioxin in those barrels—so toxic that the fatal doses were below our testing thresholds—and you're talking about it being under control?"

"Get ahold of yourself, Shelby. I'm on your side, remember?"

She took a deep breath and forced a smile. Steve was a potential ally, she reminded herself—not to mention her last great hope. There was no point in alienating him.

"You should have seen this office when we got the news three days ago," he continued, almost defensively. "We had all the makings of a first-class lynch mob."

Shelby chuckled appreciatively. "That I can relate to."

"But there are regulations we have to adhere to. These things have a rhythm all their own. It's slow—it's painfully slow sometimes—but we get the job done."

"Steve." Shelby leaned forward, her hands clenching the edge of his desk. "Dozens of whales have died. Humpbacks and even a couple of right whales, and you know how rare they are."

"I understand, Shelby. But my—the department's hands are tied. We need money, we need manpower—"

"Please, Steve. I'm not here to debate with you. All I want is for you to apply some pressure, use your influence to move the cleanup along."

Steve shook his head adamantly. "I'm a consultant, Shelby. Just a lowly grunt."

"You're my only hope, Steve. I've knocked on every door in Boston in the past thirty-six hours."

"Shelby," he began at last in a pedantic tone, "this unabashed idealism of yours is your greatest charm. It's also your greatest weakness. So, as always, let me spell out the harsh realities of life for you. Reality number one—I'm studying the long-range effects of pollutants in Boston Harbor—"

"Unlike Stellwagen Bank, Boston Harbor's been polluted for decades," Shelby interjected.

"And it may well be polluted for decades more. That's reality number two. Reality number three is that I like it here. I like my office. I like my leather chair. I like my secretary. And if I start making a pain of myself around here, they'll hand my study over to someone else, and with it my leather chair. Not to mention my secretary."

Shelby rose from her chair, fists clenched, and turned toward the door. But at the last moment she turned back. "I don't want to leave any stone unturned," she said, controlling her voice with difficulty. "I want to be absolutely sure that you will do nothing to help me."

He shook his head regretfully. "My hands are tied."

"Good. Then I've got nothing to lose," she said, reaching across his desk for his coffee mug.

Steve saw it coming, but too late.

"PAUL, I CANNOT BELIEVE what you're telling me." Jake held the receiver out, frowning at it as though the phone were the real problem. "Yes, I know government moves slowly, but—" He paused, listening with growing frustration. "Yeah, but..." Pause. "But next year! I mean, for—" He drew a deep breath and let it out in a heavy sigh. "I know you did, Paul. And I know that if you can't do it, nobody can. Still, it's rotten." He listened again, a slow smile forming on his lips.

"No, Paul. I knew Shelby was up in Boston pounding on desks, but I hadn't heard that. Dumped the whole cup in his lap?" He laughed, leaning back in the chair. "I don't suppose it did any good? No. Well, thanks, anyway, Paul."

Jake put the receiver back in its cradle and rubbed his temples. What good was it having a senator for a friend if that was the best he could do when you needed help?

It would take a year at least before a cleanup of the dump area could be started, and Richardson had emphasized that was probably an optimistic estimate. Shelby had probably run into the same roadblocks. If she was to the point of pouring coffee into the laps of bureaucrats, she was presumably stymied.

During the forty-eight hours since they had uncovered CCI's secret and turned Murphy and Marcus over to the police, Shelby had been a woman possessed, determined to leave no avenue unexplored in her quest to finally put an end to the deaths of her charges. They had scarcely exchanged a word. Was that because she was so preoccupied, or because she still felt she must distance herself from him?

Maybe when the crisis was over—but when would that be? And even when it was, would anything be different?

He felt strange, sitting in his apartment without the familiar sounds of her moving about upstairs. The night before she had stayed over in Boston, and he'd realized he couldn't get to sleep until he heard the sound of her bed creaking as she climbed into it. Would he ever again be able to get to sleep without thinking of her?

Jake knew in his heart what he had to do now, not only for Shelby, but because he also loved the sea. Yet the difficulties would be enormous, the expense crushing. It would end the salvage for the foreseeable future, and put beyond reach his own half-thought-out plan for winning back Shelby.

He glanced at his watch and stood up. The crew would be waiting for him, and he could put it off no longer. He only hoped they would understand.

SHELBY STOOD at the ocean's edge, watching the foamy surf lap at her black pumps. Vaguely she wondered how she'd ended up there.

She'd been driving home from Boston that afternoon—racing, really, actually zipping the poor old Dodge past a disgruntled Mercedes or two. But instead of turning off for home, she'd headed here, to the beach where she and Jake had watched the sun go down not so long ago.

This evening the sunset was just as gorgeous, but she wasn't in the mood to enjoy it. It seemed gaudy and excessive, given her rotten day. She'd knocked on every politico's door in Boston—even the door of the one person she'd never wanted to see again.

Funny, it was hard now to recall her old bitterness toward Steve. Why had she let herself become a prisoner of resentment toward a man who had never been cruel so much as he had just been weak?

Weak, even in his convictions.

In the end he had been far more concerned with protecting his position than in protecting the environment. She finally understood why Steve had used her the way he had:

he'd seen no alternative. Using her hard work had been his only way to move up in the world. Now, thanks to her, he had his little niche, where he could feel safe and unchallenged.

And pretty nearly useless, Shelby thought sadly. Like most of the others she'd tried to make her case to. All she'd wanted was one person to explain why it was going to take fifteen different agencies at least a year to do a few weeks' worth of cleanup work. For some reason she'd assumed she could storm the hallowed halls of government in her I-mean-business suit and heels and knock a few heads together.

Instead, she was the one with the headache, not to mention the pain her feet were in. She reached down and pulled off the uncomfortable pumps, holding them up for examination. The damp sand felt delicious in contrast.

"Shoes," she announced judiciously, "I hate you. I really do." Suddenly, flinging her arm in a wide arc, she threw them into the surf.

She stepped forward a couple of paces and allowed the chill sea to lick at her nylon-covered toes. Why weren't all life's problems so easily solved?

"Say, didn't you use to pitch for the Sox?"

Shelby started, turning to find Jake watching her from the top of a low dune. "Jake! How did you know I'd be here?"

"Just a hunch. Plus your car parked out by the road." He was barefoot, sporting his antique cutoffs and a brown T-shirt of the same vintage, and looked annoyingly complacent. "You know," he offered, joining her at the water's edge, "there are less expensive ways to take out your aggressions. Primal scream, boxing . . . sex."

"What aggressions?" she grated. "Everything's hunky-dory." Impulsively she reached for his shoulder with her right hand. "Mind if I borrow this for a minute?"

"Be my guest."

As gracefully as she could, using him to keep steady, she pulled off her nylons, rolling them into a tight ball to deposit in her purse. She met Jake's eyes sheepishly. "I shouldn't have done that with the shoes," she said, suddenly stricken with guilt. "I'm as bad as CCI."

Jake rubbed her back affectionately, and she felt a disturbingly pleasant rush of warmth through her middle. "Not quite," he reassured her. "So let me guess how things have been going. Everywhere you went you got the runaround. Nobody would give you the time of day, let alone a straight answer."

"How did you know?" she asked, ignoring the fact that she'd allowed him to reach over and begin kneading her painfully cramped neck.

"Same thing happened to me with Washington. Paul Richardson tells me a year at least, and that's if he pulls every string he can lay his hands on." He inched his fingers along her shoulders. "Boy, are you tight."

"I had a rough day."

"So did a certain ex-husband of yours, from what I hear."

"Word travels fast." She twisted around to meet his eyes, then returned her gaze to the sea. "I thought he could help, Jake," she said hesitantly. "I thought he *would* help."

She felt his massaging hands stop, then continue.

"And?" Jake asked evenly.

"And he couldn't. Or wouldn't. I don't suppose it matters which." She rolled her head forward and felt his thumbs work magic. "I'm just sorry the coffee was only lukewarm."

Jake laughed appreciatively. "You never cease to amaze me, Ms Haynes."

Shelby turned to face him. "Oh, Jake, what are we going to do? We can't let those animals die because some agency needs a year to fill out forms in triplicate."

"That's what I'm here to tell you. It's not going to take a year."

"What?" A tiny flame of hope flickered within her. "What are you saying?"

"I'm saying that some men dare to tread where bureaucrats fear to travel."

"Who, Jake? Who?" She clutched one of his hands in both of hers.

He shrugged. "One of your own. Some whale nut. Paul couldn't give me any specifics. The point is—" he stroked her hair with his free hand "—that mess out there is going to get cleaned up, and right away."

"Oh, Jake, that's wonderful!" Giddy with joy, she embraced him exuberantly until she felt his automatic response, pulling her closer with gentle insistence.

Just as gently she pulled free. It was the first time since their final lovemaking that they had touched so intimately. The feel of his hard, unyielding chest against her breasts, the familiar, manly scent of him, spicy and intoxicating, made her tremble. Her eyes brimmed with the first sting of uninvited tears, and she quickly turned her back on him, focusing on the last red remnant of sun still visible on the horizon.

"Hey," he whispered, grasping her shoulders tenderly, "you okay?"

She swept away the evidence of hot tears with her palm. "I'm fine, really. It's just—" she cleared her throat, buying time "—it's just such a relief to know everything's going to turn out all right." *Well, almost everything.*

She turned to face him again, hoping her tear-reddened eyes would go unnoticed, and forced the quaver from her voice. "So what else did the senator tell you? Who on earth could finance something like this?"

"From the sound of it, some old eccentric philanthropist with more money than brains." He kicked at a broken shell with his toe. "With the right people, it should only take a couple of weeks to clean up the mess." Hooking her chin with his index finger, he forced her to meet his gaze. "It's going to be okay, Shelby. Trust me."

She saw her own relieved expression mirrored in the black pools of his eyes. Could it be true?

"Given that this character's ready to move right away, I'm going to suspend the search for the *Evangeline* till the cleanup's over. Better safe than sorry and all that."

"So who is it?" she pressed.

"Who is who?"

"Who's paying for the cleanup?"

Jake looked off toward the sunset. "Uh, I don't know. Paul mentioned his name, but I'm not much good at remembering names. Guess that's why I'm not in politics. You need a good memory for faces and names and—"

"Well, you've got to find out. The very least we should do is tell him thanks."

"Yeah, well, I'll ask Paul next time I talk to him, although you realize the guy's probably getting a tax benefit out of it, and with the deal he and Paul worked out, the government will reimburse most of the expense."

"Now who's being cynical?" she chided. "Besides, that's not important. All that's important is that we put an end to these deaths."

"That's right," Jake agreed.

"So." Shelby looked away, shaking her head. "Thus ends the great mystery. Now we know what was killing the whales. Big surprise. It was man."

"Yes," Jake said, "and it's man who will put an end to it and punish those responsible."

"What good does punishment do for the poor animals that died?" she asked bitterly.

"None. But the next time someone like Tim Murphy tries to take the easy way out, he may think twice. As of close of market today, CCI stock had dropped thirty percent in value. Some investors are afraid there'll be expensive lawsuits and others—you might be surprised how many—are outraged by what happened. Murphy may be out on bail, but he's also out of CCI." Jake snorted derisively. "And his career prospects are dim, to say the least. It seems even the board of directors knew nothing about Murphy's little cost-cutting enterprise."

"Cost cutting?"

"Toxic waste disposal's expensive. Murphy saved CCI more than a million dollars with his illegal dumping. But with the fines and bad publicity the company faces, no one is thanking him. In fact, the CCI board is bending over backward to help put him away." He smiled disgustedly. "Maybe he and Marcus can share a cell. Marcus is cooperating for all he's worth, but he's still going to do time. Believe me, I think a very clear message has been sent."

"I know you're right," Shelby agreed. "And I have to remind myself that for every Tim Murphy, there's the kind of person who'll reach into their own pocket for a good cause and not even ask for recognition."

"Yeah, people are funny sometimes," Jake said shortly. He checked his watch. "Listen, it's about time to get back to town. I'm flying down to New York for a few days on business."

"When?" she asked, more sharply than she'd intended.

"Right away. It's just the usual stuff. My accountants like to see me in the flesh every so often and talk the almighty bottom line. It gives them something to live for." He waved toward the parking lot. "Shall we?"

"You go on, Jake. I . . . I think I'll stay for a while."

"Is your car going to start?" he joked.

"Maybe. Maybe not." Shelby sighed. "Anyway, I don't really have anywhere I have to be."

Jake hesitated, as if he'd left something unsaid. But when he finally spoke, his tone was deliberately light. "So I can safely assume you're not planning on any more pitching practice?"

"Nope." She returned his smile. "My clothes budget couldn't take the strain."

"In that case, I guess there's no point in sticking around." With a wink he trudged off slowly toward his car. A moment later she heard him pulling away.

It was true, she reflected. For the first time in a long while she felt no great urgency about getting back to work. The crisis was past, and now she was free to return to her research—and, of course, to monitoring the *Evangeline* hunt. But even her watchdogging effort had lost some of its importance now that they'd located the true danger to the whales.

What an irony that CCI, the real villain, had been a strong ally in her fight to stop a man who'd turned out to be no enemy at all. In fact, without Jake and his treasure hunt, it might have taken months, even years, to track down the problem. Dozens more whales might have died. She had fought him tooth and nail, and in the end Jake had played a very great part in averting a major catastrophe.

Still, he hadn't said, "I told you so," or demanded an apology, although Shelby knew he was entitled to one. Instead, he'd gone to his friend Richardson and done everything he could to help out. It was probably Senator Richardson who had located the philanthropist willing to finance the cleanup. A campaign contributor, no doubt, or a friend.

A friend?

Suddenly the realization hit her full force. How could she have been so blind? It had to be!

The "eccentric philanthropist with more money than brains" was Jake Lawson.

## 14

THE RITUAL WAS COMPLETE. The cup of chamomile tea, the Mozart concerto on the stereo, the steaming hot bath scented with jasmine oil.

After four nights of insomnia Shelby had developed a comforting routine to counteract the problem. If she had to play night owl, at least she was going to do it in style.

She lit the three stubby candles on the vanity and flicked off the annoying fluorescent glare of the bathroom light. Dropping her robe to the floor, she slipped a tentative toe into the sweet-smelling water. The heat made her wince.

Perfect.

Gradually she lowered herself into the tub, giving herself time to adjust to the steamy water. What she really needed was a whirlpool. Or a full-time masseur. She'd spent the last few days with her body kinked into tight little spirals, a bundle of manic energy—the perfect candidate for one of those decaffeinated coffee ads.

Each day she'd gone out to the site, supervising, or more often just watching the cleanup crew at work. Whatever Jake was doing in New York, it obviously involved the spreading around of vast sums of money.

The cleanup crew had arrived by chartered jet with their specialized equipment close on their heels. When it was discovered that there were not enough rooms available in Provincetown to accommodate the crew, four families with confirmed reservations were suddenly offered all-expenses-paid trips to Paris.

The cleanup experts worked double shifts, at a speed that suggested the lure of big bonuses for expeditious solutions. Equipment that failed was not fixed, but instantly replaced with new. State inspectors arriving to "assess" the problem were confronted with the fact that the problem was disappearing before their eyes. Their chief sheepishly admitted that at this rate the work would be done before he could submit his recommendation.

But throughout all this Jake remained absent. And no matter how happy Shelby was to see the cleanup, no matter how relieved she was that at last her charges would be safe, she felt little joy.

It was a taste of the future, Shelby realized. A sample of what life would be like when he was gone for good. For now, at least, she waited for the man. Soon she would wait only for a memory of the man.

And yet Jake must fear that as much as she. He had never denied the difficulties they faced. But, despite all that, he had risked his fortune, his hunt for the *Evangeline*, everything.

Shelby reached for her cup of tea, perched precariously on the bathtub rim, and sipped the soothing herbal brew.

He had put everything on the line. Why?

Because he loved the sea as much as she did. And because he loved *her*.

In one wild, dangerous plunge he'd put all his plans into jeopardy for the things he most loved. It had all been so reckless, with only glancing consideration for the debts he would incur, the time he would lose, the treasure that might elude his grasp. All on a wing, a prayer and one of those hunches of his that he could make it work.

*The greater the risks, the greater the rewards.*

Shelby felt a soft, sweet ache begin to swell her heart. He'd risked so much for her. As though the future didn't matter.

As though the only thing that mattered was their happiness, here, now, today.

Suddenly the throaty hum of a car engine caught her ear. She sat perfectly still, listening, as she had each of the past four long nights, for the sound she longed to hear.

A car door slammed, and through the bathroom window she heard the scrape of shoes in the driveway and the creak of the front porch door as it opened.

He was back.

Maybe Jake was right. Maybe worrying about the future only robbed the present of all joy.

Shelby reached for a bath towel and climbed from the tub. She dried herself quickly and misted her entire body in a cloud of her favorite cologne. When she looked up and glimpsed her smile in the mirror, it was radiant.

Tomorrow, or some other tomorrow, it might all end. She could see no way for them to be together. But since when was she a prophet?

In her bottom dresser drawer, amid nightgowns and oversize T-shirts, she found what she was looking for: the black lace teddy, still wrapped in tissue paper, that she had purchased on a hunch.

A hunch named Jake Lawson.

WHEN JAKE HEARD THE CLICK of the latch, for a moment he thought he was dreaming. He had collapsed into bed as soon as he'd arrived home, and it wasn't until he realized the sound might be a burglar that he forced himself back to awareness. Even then he hesitated, wondering whether there was anything in the apartment valuable enough to warrant losing sleep over.

Reluctantly he threw back the covers and climbed out of bed, all too aware that in his completely nude state he was not exactly prepared for a wrestling match with a burglar.

In the doorway he thought he could make out an indistinct, silent form. The intruder took a step forward, and all at once Jake caught the scent of orange blossoms floating on the air.

"You told me once that when I decided to come down those stairs, you'd be ready." Shelby flicked on the wall switch, and soft yellow lamplight filled the room.

Jake started to speak, but the image revealed had stunned him to incoherence.

So he *was* dreaming.

But if it was a dream, it had elicited all the physical responses of reality.

Shelby stepped closer. With each shaky inhalation the creamy orbs of her barely concealed breasts strained against a panel of sheer black lace. He saw her misted gray eyes roam the length of his body.

"Well, you're a man of your word," she murmured huskily. "You *are* ready."

He pulled her to him, tasting her parted lips, feeling her intimate heat.

"I'm not the only one," he whispered.

He trailed his hand down her abdomen until his palm cupped the heat between her thighs. Slipping his fingers boldly past the gossamer protection, his breath caught at the discovery of her petaled secrets, silky and hot and welcoming.

She smiled dreamily and moved her own hand on top of his, as if to ensure he would not stop his tender search.

The silent entreaty sent a riptide of longing through him, and when she began her own exploration, touching him daringly, he groaned out her name through clenched teeth. He sought her eyes and found them shining with a fevered luster he'd never seen before.

Jake lifted her into his arms and placed her on the downy coverlet, finding her mouth and refusing to relinquish its sweet, inviting wetness. With one hand he bared a dusky rose nipple, teasing it into arousal until the temptation was too great, and he at last released her mouth to suck there urgently, each soft little gasp from Shelby sending him closer to the edge.

When the doorbell chimed the first time, it registered only vaguely in some still-coherent corner of his mind. His only response was to peel back the lace preventing him from feasting on Shelby's other breast, too long neglected.

The bell rang again, twice this time.

"Ignore it," he commanded, lifting his head to see a smile stir on Shelby's glistening, kiss-swollen lips. He turned his attention to the velvety valley between her breasts, inhaling her lush, captivating scent.

The bell ringing was replaced by insistent pounding. "Captain!" somebody yelled. "It's important!"

"Jake," Shelby exhaled shakily. "It's all right." With trembling fingers she traced his jawline. "I can wait."

In one swift movement he slipped the teddy past her hips and down the long tanned length of her legs. "I can't," he informed her thickly.

As he pressed himself against the satiny expanse of her heated flesh, someone called out, only inches from the open bedroom window. "Captain, sir?"

Even in his distraction, he recognized the voice beyond the shade as J.B.'s.

Apparently Shelby did, too. Her eyes widened, and she bit on a knuckle, trying vainly to stifle her giggles.

Jake clenched his fists, swallowing a curse. "This better be good, J.B.," he threatened. "Damned good."

"I'm sorry, sir, really I am—"

"*Tell* him, J.B.," someone urged. "What are you waiting for, an invitation?"

"Sounds like the gang's all here," Shelby whispered, sending shudders down his spine as she lavished a trail of kisses along the taut cords of his neck.

"You'll never guess," J.B. continued loudly. "What's the most incredible thing you can imagine?"

Jake looked down at Shelby and smiled.

"Get *on* with it, J.B.!" It was Janine, sounding thoroughly exasperated.

"We just heard from the cleanup crew, Captain." Even from a distance J.B.'s excitement was obvious. "They were dredging, and they thought they'd sucked up some loose rocks—but it wasn't rocks. Captain? They were gold coins! *Gold*, Captain!"

"My God, Jake," Shelby gasped, clutching at his shoulders. "The treasure!" She moved to sit up, but he pressed her back against the comforter.

She looked beautiful there, smiling radiantly, her hair a shimmering halo around her head.

"Okay, J.B.," he murmured. "Thanks."

"But—"

"Come *on*, J.B.," Janine cut in. "Let's go celebrate, and I'll tell you all about the birds and the bees."

"*Now*, J.B." They moved away from the window, J.B.'s quizzical voice still audible in the distance.

Shelby brushed Jake's lips with a kiss. "I'm so happy for you. After all your work, all the pain, you found it. You found the treasure."

"I know," he whispered, entering her slowly, tenderly. "I know."

The first time he saw her, he'd known.

BY THE TIME SHELBY ARRIVED at the *Questor* the following day, its stern was riding a foot lower in the water, weighted down by the pile of treasure already amassed on the deck. Bars of silver as big as loaves of bread, blackened by their long stay in the water, were stacked waist-high on a wooden pallet. Masses of silver coins, fused into the shape of strongboxes, which had long since rotted away, sat immersed in washtubs. Someone had filled a gallon-size pickle jar with glittering emeralds.

But overshadowing all else was the gold, untarnished and ageless, glimmering seductively in the midday sun. Heavy gold chains, some ornamented with ruby-encrusted crosses, hung suspended on a rope clothesline. J.B. sat before a pile of gold coins, methodically separating them into buckets labeled French, Portuguese, Spanish and Other, while Thomas logged each in a notebook according to nationality and date.

Shelby lingered over all these marvels, pausing here at a silver-and-diamond goblet, there at a sapphire-studded picture frame. But inevitably her gaze was drawn, as if by some irresistible magic, back to a huge pile of gold ingots and bars, some no bigger than a man's thumb, others as large as a mailbox.

A pile, Janine had confided in an awestruck tone, they estimated to be worth nearly five million dollars.

Still, only a fraction of the treasure had been raised. CCI's barrels of waste had long since been removed, along with much of the sea floor itself. The rest of the *Evangeline*'s remains lay at the bottom of the trench, protected beneath layers of sand and silt.

"See anything you like?" Jake appeared, parting the curtain of gold chains, smiling modestly.

"That depends. What can I get for $19.95?"

"I'd say help yourself, but we can't move anything till the state auditors get here," he said. "In any case, my bankers are feeling much better."

"What a relief, Jake." She kissed him lightly on the mouth, annoyed at the melancholy that had crept into her tone.

"You sound as if the world just came to an end. This is *good* news."

"Yes, I know it is," Shelby assured him with forced gaiety. "The whales are safe now, or at least as safe as they can be. And you've found what you were looking for." Absently she lifted a thick gold chain and watched it slip through her fingers link by link. "It's been quite an adventure, hasn't it, Jake?"

He laughed. "Well, it isn't over yet."

"Isn't it?" she whispered, too softly for him to hear.

"It'll take another week to bring up the rest of the treasure."

"Another week?" she echoed bleakly. "I . . . I thought it would take longer than that."

"Normally it would, much longer. This has been an incredible stroke of luck. As well as I can reconstruct it, the *Evangeline* must have started breaking up just a half mile north of here, over where we had our first good soundings and you found Willy's snuffbox." He reached for her hand and squeezed it affectionately. "But the main holds were well constructed. They stayed together till she sank here, right above this trough. The amazing thing is that the treasure's all rather neatly collected there. It'll really simplify the excavation."

"A week." She repeated the words again, freeing her hand from Jake's grasp.

He scanned her face carefully, eyes narrowing. "Shelby, are you all right?"

"Sure," she answered dully. "Fine." She moved to the deck railing and clutched it tightly. The sea was unusually calm, an unnerving contrast to the turmoil in her heart.

She'd taken the risk, knowing things might end. It had just never occurred to her they might end so soon.

Jake joined her at the railing. "J.B. mentioned you're flying back to New York tonight," she said at last.

"Just to tie up some loose ends. My bankers want to see some proof I'm not hallucinating." He smiled. "And I've got another project on-line I want to get started on."

She heard the excitement in his voice and bit her lower lip, determined not to react. Of course he would already be planning his next exotic adventure. That was part of who Jake was, part of what she most loved about him.

But it was all ending so very, very quickly. . . .

"I'll be back late next Tuesday, near as I can figure," Jake informed her cheerfully, seemingly oblivious to her mood.

*For how long, Jake?* The silent question played in her mind like a sad refrain, but in the end it really didn't matter.

He was already gone.

SHELBY SAT on MacMillan Wharf, dangling her legs over the edge. A placid afternoon sea lapped at the huge pilings beneath her with comforting regularity. Fifty yards down the pier Cipher was serving as a one-dog welcoming committee, energetically greeting the throng of passengers just disembarking from a whale-watch tour boat.

The wharf was busy for a Wednesday, commercial fishing boats vying with pleasure craft for dock privileges. It had been quieter the day before, Shelby reflected. Tuesday. The day Jake had promised to return.

She made a halfhearted attempt to call Cipher, who ignored her in favor of an elderly couple he'd apparently befriended. "Traitor," she muttered under her breath, not entirely sure which of the males in her life she meant.

All day yesterday she'd reminded herself that Jake's imminent return would only be temporary. She was going to have to get used to life without him, and burying herself in her work seemed like a promising therapy. But somehow work seemed dull lately, less compelling than it had once been. Finding the solution to the whales' illness was part of the reason, of course: she wasn't needed the way she had been. But she suspected other things had changed her perspective, too. Things she was very much trying to forget.

That Jake hadn't returned didn't really surprise her. No doubt he wanted to find a painless way to end their relationship—as though such a thing were possible. Sailing off into the sunset was just his style.

She smiled sadly, recalling his tales of One-Arm Willy, and poor Charity left to pine away awaiting his return—a return the pirate never made.

The two men had something in common, when you got right down to it. But she was no Charity Stethem. She had to make sense of her life and move on.

Shelby stood up and called to Cipher. A shrill whistle blast pierced the air, and she looked over to see a huge new cabin cruiser slowing toward the end of the pier—another rich businessman with his expensive toy.

"Cipher, come on. Time to go," she yelled, but the dog was barking furiously, wagging his tail at the approaching yacht.

"Fine, Cipher," she said glumly, "you stay. I'll go." But as she turned away, Shelby felt an odd tingling down the length of her spine. Slowly she looked back.

Outlined in shadow on the flying bridge was a silhouette that was etched forever on her soul.

The boat's engines died, and it drifted toward the pier. J.B. appeared at the bow, calling out to her cheerfully.

"J.B.?" she said, catching the mooring line he'd tossed to her.

"Hi, Shelby. Here—" he jumped ashore and retrieved the line "—I'll get that."

"J.B., what's this all about?"

"Uh-uh, Shelby." J.B. shook his head vigorously while tying off the line. "I've had all the lectures on the birds and the bees I can take. You'll have to talk to the captain. I am outta here." He offered her a mock salute and loped off down the wharf.

Jake's shadow disappeared from the bridge, and he emerged a moment later on deck, standing several feet above her.

"Hello, love. Sorry I'm late."

"Jake?" Shelby considered several comments, discarding each in turn before finally managing, "Nice boat."

"I was hoping you'd think so. Will you come aboard?" he asked with an enigmatic smile. "And bring your furry friend."

Shelby shrugged. "Sure." She took his hand, and he hoisted her up the side.

"This thing is huge."

"Yeah, well, it had to be," Jake agreed sheepishly.

"I see." She swallowed past the hard knot in her throat. "I guess you're going after something really big next."

"You could say that. The biggest treasure of them all," he said meaningfully. "It has just about everything." He waved toward the oversize cabin. "Every technological goody a treasure hunter could ask for."

"Oh?" Shelby inquired politely, wishing she'd never climbed aboard.

"Yep." He paused, and she saw a question glowing in the ebony depths of his eyes. "It also has a completely equipped marine biological laboratory. And a king-size bed. Neither of which will be worth a damn if you're not in them."

The love in his eyes reached her heart before his words had registered there.

He was promising far more than just tomorrow. He was promising forever.

"I love you, Shelby," Jake whispered, pulling her close. "I thought . . . I hoped . . . Well, damn it, you're stuck with me, like it or not!"

"I like," she echoed.

"What did you say?"

"I said, I love you, Jake. I love you." The words were little miracles, so easy and so powerful.

Jake found her mouth, as though it were the first time, kissing her deeply, tenderly, reverently. Before them a new life together beckoned, shimmering and infinite and boundless as the sea.

"So where to now, Captain?" Shelby breathed, a rapturous smile dawning on her lips.

"I was kind of thinking of a honeymoon in Bermuda. It's beautiful there this time of year—" He hesitated, flushing beneath his tan.

"And?"

Jake grinned boyishly. "And they say there's this Spanish galleon . . ."

"That's right smack in the middle of the humpbacks' migratory route," Shelby protested.

"Really?" Jake asked innocently. "What a coincidence."

SHELBY PUT HER ARM around Jake's waist as he guided the boat into a sea ablaze with the colors of sunset. Drawn as if by instinct, she turned to look back, and as she did, a huge humpback broke the surface in a tremendous leap, arching forward and crashing back into the waves. As it dove, the broad notched tail came up, as if waving farewell.

# Harlequin Temptation

## COMING NEXT MONTH

### #233 MURPHY'S LAW JoAnn Ross

Hannah Greene had hoped for a fresh start in New Chance, Arizona, but trouble seemed to have followed her from Connecticut. It was only when Trace Murphy came to her rescue that she dared hope her luck was changing....

### #234 GYPSY Glenda Sanders

Anna Maria had left her Gypsy roots behind, but not her passionate Gypsy nature. And it didn't take much for Sheriff Thomas Banning to stir up both....

### #235 MONKEY BUSINESS Cassie Miles

Anthropologist Erica Swanson didn't want anything to interfere with the adventures she had planned for her future. But that was before she met Nick Barron...and envisioned even more exciting exploits in the here and now.

### #236 A WINNING BATTLE Carla Neggers

Christopher O. Battle, a nationally syndicated columnist, resisted the urge to lampoon a professional organizer, namely Page B. Harrington. In exchange, *she* managed to resist uncluttering his apartment. Falling in love, however, was something neither one had any control over.

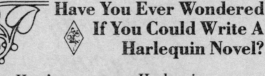

# Have You Ever Wondered If You Could Write A Harlequin Novel?

Here's great news—Harlequin is offering a series of cassette tapes to help you do just that. Written by Harlequin editors, these tapes give practical advice on how to make your characters—and your story—come alive. There's a tape for each contemporary romance series Harlequin publishes.

**Mail order only**

**All sales final**

---

# TEARS IN THE RAIN

STARRING
CHRISTOPHER CAVZENOVE AND
SHARON STONE

BASED ON A NOVEL BY
PAMELA WALLACE

PREMIERING IN NOVEMBER